Aaron Trow

The Chateau of Prince Polignac

The Courtship of Susan Bell

Aaron Trow

The Chateau of Prince Polignac

The Courtship of Susan Bell

ANTHONY TROLLOPE

Jerenity
Publishers, LLC
ROCKVILLE, MARYLAND
2009

ISBN: 978-1-60450-626-6

Published by Serenity Publishers
An Arc Manor Company
P. O. Box 10339
Rockville, MD 20849-0339
www.SerenityPublishers.com

Printed in the United States of America/United Kingdom

CONTENTS

Aaron Trow

Aaron Trow

I WOULD wish to declare, at the beginning of this story, that I shall never regard that cluster of islets which we call Bermuda as the Fortunate Islands of the ancients. Do not let professional geographers take me up, and say that no one has so accounted them, and that the ancients have never been supposed to have gotten themselves so far westwards. What I mean to assert is this—that, had any ancient been carried thither by enterprise or stress of weather, he would not have given those islands so good a name. That the Neapolitan sailors of King Alonzo should have been wrecked here, I consider to be more likely. The vexed Bermoothes is a good name for them. There is no getting in or out of them without the greatest difficulty, and a patient, slow navigation, which is very heart-rending. That Caliban should have lived here I can imagine; that Ariel would have been sick of the place is certain; and that Governor Prospero should have been willing to abandon his governorship, I conceive to have been only natural. When one regards the present state of the place, one is tempted to doubt whether any of the governors have been conjurors since his days.

Bermuda, as all the world knows, is a British colony at which we maintain a convict establishment. Most of our outlying convict establishments have been sent back upon our hands from our colonies, but here one is still maintained. There is also in the islands a strong military fortress, though not a fortress looking magnificent to the eyes of civilians, as do Malta and Gibraltar. There are also here some six thousand white people and some six thousand black people, eating, drinking, sleeping, and dying.

The convict establishment is the most notable feature of Bermuda to a stranger, but it does not seem to attract much attention from the regular inhabitants of the place. There is no intercourse between the prisoners and the Bermudians. The convicts are rarely seen by them, and the convict islands are rarely visited. As to the prisoners themselves, of course it is not open to them—or should not be open to them—to have intercourse with any but the prison authorities.

There have, however, been instances in which convicts have escaped from their confinement, and made their way out among the islands. Poor wretches! As a rule, there is but little chance for any that can so escape. The whole length of the cluster is but twenty miles, and the breadth is under four. The prisoners are, of course, white men, and the lower orders of Bermuda, among whom alone could a runagate have any chance of hiding himself, are all negroes; so that such a one would be known at once. Their clothes are all marked. Their only chance of a permanent escape would be in the hold of an American ship; but what captain of an American or other ship would willingly encumber himself with an escaped convict? But, nevertheless, men have escaped; and in one instance, I believe, a convict got away, so that of him no farther tidings were ever heard.

For the truth of the following tale I will not by any means vouch. If one were to inquire on the spot one might probably find that the ladies all believe it, and the old men; that all the young men know exactly how much of it is false and how much true; and that the steady, middle-aged, well-to-do islanders are quite convinced that it is romance from beginning to end. My readers may range themselves with the ladies, the young men, or the steady, well-to-do, middle-aged islanders, as they please.

Some years ago, soon after the prison was first established on its present footing, three men did escape from it, and among them a certain notorious prisoner named Aaron Trow. Trow's antecedents in England had not been so villanously bad as those of many of his fellow-convicts, though the one offence for which he was punished had been of a deep dye: he had shed man's blood. At a period of great distress in a manufacturing town he had led men on to riot, and with his own hand had slain the first constable who had endeavoured to do his duty against him. There had been courage in the doing of the deed, and probably no malice; but the deed, let its moral blackness have been what it might, had sent him to Bermuda, with a sentence against him of penal servitude for life. Had he been then amenable to prison discipline,—even then, with such a sentence against him as that,—he might have won his way back, after the lapse of years, to the children, and perhaps, to the wife, that he had left behind him; but he was amenable to no rules—to no discipline. His heart was sore to death with an idea of injury, and he lashed himself against the bars of his cage with a feeling that it would be well if he could so lash himself till he might perish in his fury.

And then a day came in which an attempt was made by a large body of convicts, under his leadership, to get the better of the officers of the prison. It is hardly necessary to say that the attempt failed. Such attempts always fail. It failed on this occasion signally, and Trow, with two other men, were condemned to be scourged terribly, and then kept in solitary confinement for some lengthened term of months. Before, however, the day of scourging came, Trow and his two associates had escaped.

I have not the space to tell how this was effected, nor the power to describe the manner. They did escape from the establishment into the islands, and though two of them were taken after a single day's run at liberty, Aaron Trow had not been yet retaken even when a week was over. When a month was over he had not been retaken, and the officers of the prison began to say that he had got away from them in a vessel to the States. It was impossible, they said, that he should have remained in the islands and not been discovered. It was not impossible that he might have destroyed himself, leaving his body where it had not yet been found. But he could not have lived on in Bermuda during that month's search. So, at least, said the officers of the prison. There was, however, a report through the islands that he had been seen from time to time; that he had gotten bread from the negroes at night, threatening them with death if they told of his whereabouts; and that all the clothes of the mate of a vessel had been stolen while the man was bathing, including a suit of dark blue cloth, in which suit of clothes, or in one of such a nature, a stranger had been seen skulking about the rocks near St. George. All this the governor of the prison affected to disbelieve, but the opinion was becoming very rife in the islands that Aaron Trow was still there.

A vigilant search, however, is a task of great labour, and cannot be kept up for ever. By degrees it was relaxed. The warders and gaolers ceased to patrol the island roads by night, and it was agreed that Aaron Trow was gone, or that he would be starved to death, or that he would in time be driven to leave such traces of his whereabouts as must lead to his discovery; and this at last did turn out to be the fact.

There is a sort of prettiness about these islands which, though it never rises to the loveliness of romantic scenery, is nevertheless attractive in its way. The land breaks itself into little knolls, and the sea runs up, hither and thither, in a thousand creeks and inlets; and then, too, when the oleanders are in bloom, they give a wonderfully bright colour to the landscape. Oleanders seem to be the roses of Bermuda, and are cultivated round all the villages of the better class through the islands. There are two towns, St. George and Hamilton, and one main high-road, which connects them; but even this high-road is broken by a ferry, over which every vehicle going from St. George to Hamilton must be conveyed. Most of the locomotion in these parts is done by boats, and the residents look to the sea, with its narrow creeks, as their best highway from their farms to their best market. In those days—and those days were not very long since—the building of small ships was their chief trade, and they valued their land mostly for the small scrubby cedar-trees with which this trade was carried on.

As one goes from St. George to Hamilton the road runs between two seas; that to the right is the ocean; that on the left is an inland creek, which runs up through a large portion of the islands, so that the land on the other side of it is near to the traveller. For a considerable portion of the way there are no houses lying near the road, and, there is one residence, some way from the road, so secluded that no other house lies within a mile of it by land. By water it might probably be reached within half a mile. This place was called Crump Island, and here lived, and had lived for many years, an old gentleman, a native of Bermuda, whose business it had been to buy up cedar wood and sell it to the ship-builders at Hamilton. In our story we shall not have very much to do with old Mr. Bergen, but it will be necessary to say a word or two about his house.

It stood upon what would have been an island in the creek, had not a narrow causeway, barely broad enough for a road, joined it to that larger island on which stands the town of St. George. As the main road approaches the ferry it runs through some rough, hilly, open ground, which on the right side towards the ocean has never been cultivated. The distance from the ocean here may, perhaps, be a quarter of a mile, and the ground is for the most part covered with low furze. On the left of the road the land is cultivated in patches, and here, some half mile or more from the ferry, a path turns away to Crump Island. The house cannot be seen from the road, and, indeed, can hardly be seen at all, except from the sea. It lies, perhaps, three furlongs from the high road, and the path to it is but little used, as the passage to and from it is chiefly made by water.

Here, at the time of our story, lived Mr. Bergen, and here lived Mr. Bergen's daughter. Miss Bergen was well known at St. George's as a steady, good girl, who spent her time in looking after her father's household matters, in managing his two black maid-servants and the black gardener, and who did her duty in that sphere of life to which she had been called. She was a comely, well-shaped young woman, with a sweet countenance, rather large in size, and very quiet in demeanour. In her earlier years, when young girls usually first bud forth into womanly beauty, the neighbours had not thought much of Anastasia Bergen, nor had the young men of St. George been wont to stay their boats under the window of Crump Cottage in order that they might listen to her voice or feel the light of her eye; but slowly, as years went by, Anastasia Bergen became a woman that a man might well love; and a man learned to love her who was well worthy of a woman's heart. This was Caleb Morton, the Presbyterian minister of St. George; and Caleb Morton had been engaged to marry Miss Bergen for the last two years past, at the period of Aaron Trow's escape from prison.

Caleb Morton was not a native of Bermuda, but had been sent thither by the synod of his church from Nova Scotia. He was a tall, handsome man, at this time of some thirty years of age, of a presence which might almost have been called commanding. He was very strong, but of a temperament which did not often give him opportunity to put forth his strength; and his life had been such that neither he nor others knew of what nature might be his courage. The greater part of his life was spent in preaching to some few of the white people around him, and in teaching as many of the blacks as he could get to hear him. His days were very quiet, and had been altogether without excitement until he had met with Anastasia Bergen. It will suffice for us to say that he did meet her, and that now, for two years past, they had been engaged as man and wife.

Old Mr. Bergen, when he heard of the engagement, was not well pleased at the information. In the first place, his daughter was very necessary to him, and the idea of her marrying and going away had hardly as yet occurred to him; and then he was by no means inclined to part with any of his money. It must not be presumed that he had amassed a fortune by his trade in cedar wood. Few tradesmen in Bermuda do, as I imagine, amass fortunes. Of some few hundred pounds he was possessed, and these, in the course of nature, would go to his daughter when he died; but he had no inclination to hand any portion of them over to his daughter before they did go to her in the course of nature. Now, the income which Caleb Morton earned as a Presbyterian clergyman was not large, and, therefore, no day had been fixed as yet for his marriage with Anastasia.

But, though the old man had been from the first averse to the match, his hostility had not been active. He had not forbidden Mr. Morton his house, or affected to be in any degree angry because his daughter had a lover. He had merely grumbled forth an intimation that those who marry in haste repent at leisure,—that love kept nobody warm if the pot did not boil; and that, as for him, it was as much as he could do to keep his own pot boiling at Crump Cottage. In answer to this Anastasia said nothing. She asked him for no money, but still kept his accounts, managed his household, and looked patiently forward for better days.

Old Mr. Bergen himself spent much of his time at Hamilton, where he had a woodyard with a couple of rooms attached to it. It was his custom to remain here three nights of the week, during which Anastasia was left alone at the cottage; and it happened by no means seldom that she was altogether alone, for the negro whom they called the gardener would go to her father's place at Hamilton, and the two black girls would crawl away up to the road, tired with the monotony of the sea at the cottage. Caleb had more than once told her that she was too much alone, but she had laughed at him, saying that solitude in Bermuda was not dangerous. Nor, indeed, was it; for the people are quiet and well-mannered, lacking much energy, but being, in the same degree, free from any propensity to violence.

"So you are going," she said to her lover, one evening, as he rose from the chair on which he had been swinging himself at the door of the cottage which looks down over the creek of the sea. He had sat there for an hour talking to her as she worked, or watching her as she moved about the place. It was a beautiful evening, and the sun had been falling to rest with almost tropical glory before his feet. The bright oleanders were red with their blossoms all around him, and he had thoroughly enjoyed his hour of easy rest. "So you are going," she said to him, not putting her work out of her hand as he rose to depart.

"Yes; and it is time for me to go. I have still work to do before I can get to bed. Ah, well; I suppose the day will come at last when I need not leave you as soon as my hour of rest is over."

"Come; of course it will come. That is, if your reverence should choose to wait for it another ten years or so."

"I believe you would not mind waiting twenty years."

"Not if a certain friend of mine would come down and see me of evenings when I'm alone after the day. It seems to me that I shouldn't mind waiting as long as I had that to look for."

"You are right not to be impatient," he said to her, after a pause, as he held her hand before he went. "Quite right. I only wish I could school myself to be as easy about it."

"I did not say I was easy," said Anastasia. "People are seldom easy in this world, I take it. I said I could be patient. Do not look in that way, as though you pretended that you were dissatisfied with me. You know that I am true to you, and you ought to be very proud of me."

"I am proud of you, Anastasia—" on hearing which she got up and courtesied to him. "I am proud of you; so proud of you that I feel you should not be left here all alone, with no one to help you if you were in trouble."

"Women don't get into trouble as men do, and do not want any one to help them. If you were alone in the house you would have to go to bed without your supper, because you could not make a basin of boiled milk ready for your own meal. Now, when your reverence has gone, I shall go to work and have my tea comfortably." And then he did go, bidding God bless her as he left her. Three hours after that he was disturbed in his own lodgings by one of the negro girls from the cottage rushing to his door, and begging him in Heaven's name to come down to the assistance of her mistress.

When Morton left her, Anastasia did not proceed to do as she had said, and seemed to have forgotten her evening meal. She had been working sedulously with her needle during all that last conversation; but when her lover was gone, she allowed the work to fall from her hands, and sat motionless for awhile, gazing at the last streak of colour left by the setting sun; but there was no longer a sign of its glory to be traced in the heavens around her. The twilight in Bermuda is not long and enduring as it is with us, though the daylight does not depart suddenly, leaving the darkness of night behind it without any intermediate time of warning, as is the case farther south, down among the islands of the tropics. But the soft, sweet light of the evening had waned and gone, and night had absolutely come upon her, while Anastasia was still seated before the cottage with her eyes fixed upon the white streak of motionless sea which was still visible through the gloom. She was thinking of him, of his ways of life, of his happiness, and of her duty towards him. She had told him, with her pretty feminine falseness, that she could wait without impatience; but now she said to herself that it would not be good for him to wait longer. He lived alone and without comfort, working very hard for his poor pittance, and she could see, and feel, and understand that a companion in his life was to him almost a necessity. She would tell her father that all this must be brought to an end. She would not ask him for money, but she would make him understand that her services must, at any rate in part, be transferred. Why should not she and Morton still live at the cottage when they were married? And so thinking, and at last resolving, she sat there till the dark night fell upon her.

She was at last disturbed by feeling a man's hand upon her shoulder. She jumped from her chair and faced him,—not screaming, for it was especially within her power to control herself, and to make no utterance except with forethought. Perhaps it might have been better for her had she screamed, and sent a shrill shriek down the shore of that inland sea. She was silent, however, and with awe-struck face and outstretched hands gazed into the face of him who still held her by the shoulder. The night was dark; but her eyes were now accustomed to the darkness, and she could see indistinctly something of his features. He was a low-sized man, dressed in a suit of sailor's blue clothing, with a rough cap of hair on his head, and a beard that had not been clipped for many weeks. His eyes were large, and hollow, and frightfully bright, so that she seemed to see nothing else of him; but she felt the strength of his fingers as he grasped her tighter and more tightly by the arm.

"Who are you?" she said, after a moment's pause.

"Do you know me?" he asked.

"Know you! No." But the words were hardly out of her mouth before it struck her that the man was Aaron Trow, of whom every one in Bermuda had been talking.

"Come into the house," he said, "and give me food." And he still held her with his hand as though he would compel her to follow him.

She stood for a moment thinking what she would say to him; for even then, with that terrible man standing close to her in the darkness, her presence of mind did not desert her. "Surely," she said, "I will give you food if you are hungry. But take your hand from me. No man would lay his hands on a woman."

"A woman!" said the stranger. "What does the starved wolf care for that? A woman's blood is as sweet to him as that of a man. Come into the house, I tell you." And then she preceded him through the open door into the narrow passage, and thence to the kitchen. There she saw that the back door, leading out on the other side of the house, was open, and she knew that he had come down from the road and entered on that side. She threw her eyes around, looking for the negro girls; but they were away, and she remembered that there was no human being within sound of her voice but this man who had told her that he was as a wolf thirsty after her blood!

"Give me food at once," he said.

"And will you go if I give it you?" she asked.

"I will knock out your brains if you do not," he replied, lifting from the grate a short, thick poker which lay there. "Do as I bid you at once. You also would be like a tiger if you had fasted for two days, as I have done."

She could see, as she moved across the kitchen, that he had already searched there for something that he might eat, but that he had searched in vain. With the close economy common among his class in the islands, all comestibles were kept under close lock and key in the house of Mr. Bergen. Their daily allowance was given day by day to the negro servants, and even the fragments were then gathered up and locked away in safety. She moved across the kitchen to the accustomed cupboard, taking the keys from her pocket, and he followed close upon her. There was a small oil lamp hanging from the low ceiling which just gave them light to see each other. She lifted her hand to this to tare it from its hook, but he prevented her. "No, by Heaven!" he said, "you don't touch that till I've done with it. There's light enough for you to drag out your scraps."

She did drag out her scraps and a bowl of milk, which might hold perhaps a quart. There was a fragment of bread, a morsel of cold potato-cake, and the bone of a leg of kid. "And is that all?" said he. But as he spoke he fleshed his teeth against the bone as a dog would have done.

"It is the best I have," she said; "I wish it were better, and you should have had it without violence, as you have suffered so long from hunger."

"Bah! Better; yes! You would give the best no doubt, and set the hell hounds on my track the moment I am gone. I know how much I might expect from your charity."

"I would have fed you for pity's sake," she answered.

"Pity! Who are you, that you should dare to pity me! By -, my young woman, it is I that pity you. I must cut your throat unless you give me money. Do you know that?"

"Money! I have got no money."

"I'll make you have some before I go. Come; don't move till I have done." And as he spoke to her he went on tugging at the bone, and swallowing the lumps of stale bread. He had already finished the bowl of milk. "And, now," said he, "tell me who I am."

"I suppose you are Aaron Trow," she answered, very slowly. He said nothing on hearing this, but continued his meal, standing close to her so that she might not possibly escape from him out into the darkness. Twice or thrice in those few minutes she made up her mind to make such an attempt, feeling that it would be better to leave him in possession of the house, and make sure, if possible, of her own life. There was no money there; not a dollar! What money her father kept in his possession was locked up in his safe at Hamilton. And might he not keep to his threat, and murder her, when he found that she could give him nothing? She did not tremble outwardly, as she stood there watching him as he ate, but she thought how probable it might be that her last moments were very near. And yet she could scrutinise his features, form, and garments, so as to carry away in her mind a perfect picture of them. Aaron Trow—for of course it was the escaped convict—was not a man of frightful, hideous aspect. Had the world used him well, giving him when he was young ample wages and separating him from turbulent spirits, he also might have used the world well; and then women would have praised the brightness of his eye and the manly vigour of his brow. But things had not gone well with him. He had been separated from the wife he had loved, and the children who had been raised at his knee,—separated by his own violence; and now, as he had said of himself, he was a wolf rather than a man. As he stood there satisfying the craving of his appetite, breaking up the large morsels of food, he was an object very sad to be seen. Hunger had made him gaunt and yellow, he was squalid with the dirt of his hidden lair, and he had the look of a beast;—that look to which men fall when they live like the brutes of prey, as outcasts from their brethren. But still there was that about his brow which might have redeemed him,—which might have turned her horror into pity, had he been willing that it should be so.

"And now give me some brandy," he said.

There was brandy in the house,—in the sitting-room which was close at their hand, and the key of the little press which held it was in her pocket. It was useless, she thought, to refuse him; and so she told him that there was a bottle partly full, but that she must go to the next room to fetch it him.

"We'll go together, my darling," he said. "There's nothing like good company." And he again put his hand upon her arm as they passed into the family sitting-room.

"I must take the light," she said. But he unhooked it himself, and carried it in his own hand.

Again she went to work without trembling. She found the key of the side cupboard, and unlocking the door, handed him a bottle which might contain about half-a-pint of spirits. "And is that all?" he said.

"There is a full bottle here," she answered, handing him another; "but if you drink it, you will be drunk, and they will catch you."

"By Heavens, yes; and you would be the first to help them; would you not?"

"Look here," she answered. "If you will go now, I will not say a word to any one of your coming, nor set them on your track to follow you. There, take the full bottle with you. If you will go, you shall be safe from me."

"What, and go without money!"

"I have none to give you. You may believe me when I say so. I have not a dollar in the house."

Before he spoke again he raised the half empty bottle to his mouth, and drank as long as there was a drop to drink. "There," said he, putting the bottle down, "I am better after that. As to the other, you are right, and I will take it with me. And now, young woman, about the money?"

"I tell you that I have not a dollar."

"Look here," said he, and he spoke now in a softer voice, as though he would be on friendly terms with her. "Give me ten sovereigns, and I will go. I know you have it, and with ten sovereigns it is possible that I may save my life. You are good, and would not wish that a man should die so horrid a death. I know you are good. Come, give me the money." And he put his hands up, beseeching her, and looked into her face with imploring eyes.

"On the word of a Christian woman I have not got money to give you," she replied.

"Nonsense?" And as he spoke he took her by the arm and shook her. He shook her violently so that he hurt her, and her breath for a moment was all but gone from her. "I tell you you must make dollars before I leave you, or I will so handle you that it would have been better for you to coin your very blood."

"May God help me at my need," she said, "as I have not above a few penny pieces in the house."

"And you expect me to believe that! Look here! I will shake the teeth out of your head, but I will have it from you." And he did shake her again, using both his hands and striking her against the wall.

"Would you—murder me?" she said, hardly able now to utter the words.

"Murder you, yes; why not? I cannot be worse than I am, were I to murder you ten times over. But with money I may possibly be better."

"I have it not."

"Then I will do worse than murder you. I will make you such an object that all the world shall loathe to look on you." And so saying he took her by the arm and dragged her forth from the wall against which she had stood.

Then there came from her a shriek that was heard far down the shore of that silent sea, and away across to the solitary houses of those living on the other side,—a shriek, very sad, sharp, and prolonged,—which told plainly to those who heard it of woman's woe when in her extremest peril. That sound was spoken of in Bermuda for many a day after that, as something which had been terrible to hear. But then, at that moment, as it came wailing through the dark, it sounded as though it were not human. Of those who heard it, not one guessed from whence it came, nor was the hand of any brother put forward to help that woman at her need.

"Did you hear that?" said the young wife to her husband, from the far side of the arm of the sea.

"Hear it! Oh Heaven, yes! Whence did it come?" The young wife could not say from whence it came, but clung close to her husband's breast, comforting herself with the knowledge that that terrible sorrow was not hers.

But aid did come at last, or rather that which seemed as aid. Long and terrible was the fight between that human beast of prey and the poor victim which had fallen into his talons. Anastasia Bergen was a strong, well-built woman, and now that the time had come to her when a struggle was necessary, a struggle for life, for honour, for the happiness of him who was more to her than herself, she fought like a tigress attacked in her own lair. At such a moment as this she also could become wild and savage as the beast of the forest. When he pinioned her arms with one of his, as he pressed her down upon the floor, she caught the first joint of the forefinger of his other hand between her teeth till he yelled in agony, and another sound was heard across the silent water. And then, when one hand was loosed in the struggle, she twisted it through his long hair, and dragged back his head till his eyes were nearly starting from their sockets. Anastasia Bergen had hitherto been a sheer woman, all feminine in her nature. But now the foam came to her mouth, and fire sprang from her eyes, and the muscles of her body worked as though she had been trained to deeds of violence. Of violence, Aaron Trow had known much in his rough life, but never had he combated with harder antagonist than her whom he now held beneath his breast.

"By—I will put an end to you," he exclaimed, in his wrath, as he struck her violently across the face with his elbow. His hand was occupied, and he could not use it for a blow, but, nevertheless, the violence was so great that the blood gushed from her nostrils, while the back of her head was driven with violence against the floor. But she did not lose her hold of him. Her hand was still twined closely through his thick hair, and in every move he made she clung to him with all her might. "Leave go my hair," he shouted at her, but she still kept her hold, though he again dashed her head against the floor.

There was still light in the room, for when he first grasped her with both his hands, he had put the lamp down on a small table. Now they were rolling on the floor together, and twice he had essayed to kneel on her that he might thus crush the breath from her body, and deprive her altogether of her strength; but she had been too active for him, moving herself along the ground, though in doing so she dragged him with her. But by degrees he got one hand at liberty, and with that he pulled a clasp knife out of his pocket and opened it. "I will cut your head off if you do not let go my hair," he said. But still she held fast by him. He then stabbed at her arm, using his left hand and making short, ineffectual blows. Her dress partly saved her, and partly also the continual movement of all her limbs; but, nevertheless, the knife wounded her. It wounded her in several places about the arm, covering them both with blood;—but still she hung on. So close was her grasp in her agony, that, as she afterwards found, she cut the skin of her own hands with her own nails. Had the man's hair been less thick or strong, or her own tenacity less steadfast, he would have murdered her before any interruption could have saved her.

And yet he had not purposed to murder her, or even, in the first instance, to inflict on her any bodily harm. But he had been determined to get money. With such a sum of money as he had named, it might, he thought, be possible for him to win his way across to America.

He might bribe men to hide him in the hold of a ship, and thus there might be for him, at any rate, a possibility of escape. That there must be money in the house he had still thought when first he laid hands on the poor woman; and then, when the struggle had once begun, when he had felt her muscles contending with his, the passion of the beast was aroused within him, and he strove against her as he would have striven against a dog. But yet, when the knife was in his hand, he had not driven it against her heart.

Then suddenly, while they were yet rolling on the floor, there was a sound of footsteps in the passage. Aaron Trow instantly leaped to his feet, leaving his victim on the ground, with huge lumps of his thick clotted hair in her hand. Thus, and thus only, could he have liberated himself from her grasp. He rushed at the door, and there he came against the two negro servant-girls who had returned down to their kitchen from the road on which they had been straying. Trow, as he half saw them in the dark, not knowing how many there might be, or whether there was a man among them, rushed through them, upsetting one scared girl in his passage. With the instinct and with the timidity of a beast, his impulse now was to escape, and he hurried away back to the road and to his lair, leaving the three women together in the cottage. Poor wretch! As he crossed the road, not skulking in his impotent haste, but running at his best, another pair of eyes saw him, and when the search became hot after him, it was known that his hiding-place was not distant.

It was some time before any of the women were able to act, and when some step was taken, Anastasia was the first to take it. She had not absolutely swooned, but the reaction, after the violence of her efforts, was so great, that for some minutes she had been unable to speak. She had risen from the floor when Trow left her, and had even followed him to the door; but since that she had fallen back into her father's old arm-chair, and there sat gasping not only for words, but for breath also.

At last she bade one of the girls to run into St. George, and beg Mr. Morton to come to her aid. The girl would not stir without her companion; and even then, Anastasia, covered as she was with blood, with dishevelled hair, and her clothes half torn from her body, accompanied them as far as the road. There they found a negro lad still hanging about the place, and he told them that he had seen the man cross the road, and run down over the open ground towards the rocks of the sea-coast. "He must be there," said the lad, pointing in the direction of a corner of the rocks; "unless he swim across the mouth of the ferry." But the mouth of that ferry is an arm of the sea, and it was not probable that a man would do that when he might have taken the narrow water by keeping on the other side of the road.

At about one that night Caleb Morton reached the cottage breathless with running, and before a word was spoken between them, Anastasia had fallen on his shoulder and had fainted. As soon as she was in the arms of her lover, all her power had gone from her. The spirit and passion of the tiger had gone, and she was again a weak woman shuddering at the thought of what she had suffered. She remembered that she had had the man's hand between her teeth, and by degrees she found his hair still clinging to her fingers; but even then she could hardly call to mind the nature of the struggle she had undergone. His hot breath close to her own cheek she did remember, and his glaring eyes, and even the roughness of his beard as he pressed his face against her own; but she could

ANTHONY TROLLOPE

not say whence had come the blood, nor till her arm
became stiff and motionless did she know that she
had been wounded.

It was all joy with her now, as she sat motionless without speaking, while he administered to her wants and
spoke words of love into her ears. She remembered the
man's horrid threat, and knew that by God's mercy she
had been saved. And he was there caressing her, lov-
ing her, comforting her! As she thought of the fate that
had threatened her, of the evil that had been so immi-
nent, she fell forward on her knees, and with incoher-
ent sobs uttered her thanksgivings, while her head was
still supported on his arms.

It was almost morning before she could induce herself
to leave him and lie down. With him she seemed to
be so perfectly safe; but the moment he was away she
could see Aaron Trow's eyes gleaming at her across the
room. At last, however, she slept; and when he saw that
she was at rest, he told himself that his work must then
begin. Hitherto Caleb Morton had lived in all respects
the life of a man of peace; but now, asking himself no
questions as to the propriety of what he would do, using no inward arguments as to this or that line of conduct, he girded the sword on his loins, and prepared
himself for war. The wretch who had thus treated the
woman whom he loved should be hunted down like a
wild beast, as long as he had arms and legs with which
to carry on the hunt. He would pursue the miscreant
with any weapons that might come to his hands; and
might Heaven help him at his need as he dealt forth
punishment to that man, if he caught him within his
grasp. Those who had hitherto known Morton in the
island, could not recognise the man as he came forth
on that day, thirsty after blood, and desirous to thrust
himself into personal conflict with the wild ruffian

who had injured him. The meek Presbyterian minister had been a preacher, preaching ways of peace, and living in accordance with his own doctrines. The world had been very quiet for him, and he had walked quietly in his appointed path. But now the world was quiet no longer, nor was there any preaching of peace. His cry was for blood; for the blood of the untamed savage brute who had come upon his young doe in her solitude, and striven with such brutal violence to tear her heart from her bosom.

He got to his assistance early in the morning some of the constables from St. George, and before the day was over, he was joined by two or three of the warders from the convict establishment. There was with him also a friend or two, and thus a party was formed, numbering together ten or twelve persons. They were of course all armed, and therefore it might be thought that there would be but small chance for the wretched man if they should come upon his track. At first they all searched together, thinking from the tidings which had reached them that he must be near to them; but gradually they spread themselves along the rocks between St. George and the ferry, keeping watchman on the road, so that he should not escape unnoticed into the island.

Ten times during the day did Anastasia send from the cottage up to Morton, begging him to leave the search to others, and come down to her. But not for a moment would he lose the scent of his prey. What! should it be said that she had been so treated, and that others had avenged her? He sent back to say that her father was with her now, and that he would come when his work was over. And in that job of work the life-blood of Aaron Trow was counted up.

ANTHONY TROLLOPE

Towards evening they were all congregated on the road near to the spot at which the path turns off towards the cottage, when a voice was heard hallooing to them from the summit of a little hill which lies between the road and the sea on the side towards the ferry, and presently a boy came running down to them full of news. "Danny Lund has seen him," said the boy, "he has seen him plainly in among the rocks." And then came Danny Lund himself, a small negro lad about fourteen years of age, who was known in those parts as the idlest, most dishonest, and most useless of his race. On this occasion, however, Danny Lund became important, and every one listened to him. He had seen, he said, a pair of eyes moving down in a cave of the rocks which he well knew. He had been in the cave often, he said, and could get there again. But not now; not while that pair of eyes was moving at the bottom of it. And so they all went up over the hill, Morton leading the way with hot haste. In his waist-band he held a pistol, and his hand grasped a short iron bar with which he had armed himself. They ascended the top of the hill, and when there, the open sea was before them on two sides, and on the third was the narrow creek over which the ferry passed. Immediately beneath their feet were the broken rocks; for on that side, towards the sea, the earth and grass of the hill descended but a little way towards the water. Down among the rocks they all went, silently, Caleb Morton leading the way, and Danny Lund directing him from behind.

"Mr. Morton," said an elderly man from St. George, "had you not better let the warders of the gaol go first; he is a desperate man, and they will best understand his ways?"

In answer to this Morton said nothing, but he would let no one put a foot before him. He still pressed forward among the rocks, and at last came to a spot from whence he might have sprung at one leap into the ocean. It was a broken cranny on the sea-shore into which the sea beat, and surrounded on every side but the one by huge broken fragments of stone, which at first sight seemed as though they would have admitted of a path down among them to the water's edge; but which, when scanned more closely, were seen to be so large in size, that no man could climb from one to another. It was a singularly romantic spot, but now well known to them all there, for they had visited it over and over again that morning.

"In there," said Danny Lund, keeping well behind Morton's body, and pointing at the same time to a cavern high up among the rocks, but quite on the opposite side of the little inlet of the sea. The mouth of the cavern was not twenty yards from where they stood, but at the first sight it seemed as though it must be impossible to reach it. The precipice on the brink of which they all now stood, ran down sheer into the sea, and the fall from the mouth of the cavern on the other side was as steep. But Danny solved the mystery by pointing upwards, and showing them how he had been used to climb to a projecting rock over their heads, and from thence creep round by certain vantages of the stone till he was able to let himself down into the aperture. But now, at the present moment, he was unwilling to make essay of his prowess as a cragsman. He had, he said, been up on that projecting rock thrice, and there had seen the eyes moving in the cavern. He was quite sure of that fact of the pair of eyes, and declined to ascend the rock again.

Traces soon became visible to them by which they knew that some one had passed in and out of the cavern recently. The stone, when examined, bore those marks of friction which passage and repassage over it will always give. At the spot from whence the climber left the platform and commenced his ascent, the side of the stone had been rubbed by the close friction of a man's body. A light boy like Danny Lund might find his way in and out without leaving such marks behind him, but no heavy man could do so. Thus before long they all were satisfied that Aaron Trow was in the cavern before them.

Then there was a long consultation as to what they would do to carry on the hunt, and how they would drive the tiger from his lair. That he should not again come out, except to fall into their hands, was to all of them a matter of course. They would keep watch and ward there, though it might be for days and nights. But that was a process which did not satisfy Morton, and did not indeed well satisfy any of them. It was not only that they desired to inflict punishment on the miscreant in accordance with the law, but also that they did not desire that the miserable man should die in a hole like a starved dog, and that then they should go after him to take out his wretched skeleton. There was something in that idea so horrid in every way, that all agreed that active steps must be taken. The warders of the prison felt that they would all be disgraced if they could not take their prisoner alive. Yet who would get round that perilous ledge in the face of such an adversary? A touch to any man while climbing there would send him headlong down among the wave! And then his fancy told to each what might be the nature of an embrace with such an animal as that, driven to despair, hopeless of life, armed, as they knew, at any rate, with a knife! If the first adventurous spirit should succeed in crawling round that ledge, what would be the reception which he might expect in the terrible depth of that cavern?

They called to their prisoner, bidding him come out, and telling him that they would fire in upon him if he did not show himself; but not a sound was heard. It was indeed possible that they should send their bullets to, perhaps, every corner of the cavern; and if so, in that way they might slaughter him; but even of this they were not sure. Who could tell that there might not be some protected nook in which he could lay secure? And who could tell when the man was struck, or whether he were wounded?

"I will get to him," said Morton, speaking with a low dogged voice, and so saying he clambered up to the rock to which Danny Lund had pointed. Many voices at once attempted to restrain him, and one or two put their hands upon him to keep him back, but he was too quick for them, and now stood upon the ledge of rock. "Can you see him?" they asked below.

"I can see nothing within the cavern," said Morton.

"Look down very hard, Massa," said Danny, "very hard indeed, down in deep dark hole, and then see him big eyes moving!"

Morton now crept along the ledge, or rather he was beginning to do so, having put forward his shoulders and arms to make a first step in advance from the spot on which he was resting, when a hand was put forth from one corner of the cavern's mouth,—a hand armed with a pistol;—and a shot was fired. There could be no doubt now but that Danny Lund was right, and no doubt now as to the whereabouts of Aaron Trow.

A hand was put forth, a pistol was fired, and Caleb Morton still clinging to a corner of the rock with both his arms was seen to falter. "He is wounded," said one of the voices from below; and then they all expected to see him fall into the sea. But he did not fall, and after a moment or two, he proceeded carefully to pick his steps along the ledge. The ball had touched him, grazing his cheek, and cutting through the light whiskers that he wore; but he had not felt it, though the blow had nearly knocked him from his perch. And then four or five shots were fired from the rocks into the mouth of the cavern. The man's arm had been seen, and indeed one or two declared that they had traced the dim outline of his figure. But no sound was heard to come from the cavern, except the sharp crack of the bullets against the rock, and the echo of the gunpowder. There had been no groan as of a man wounded, no sound of a body falling, no voice wailing in despair. For a few seconds all was dark with the smoke of the gunpowder, and then the empty mouth of the cave was again yawning before their eyes. Morton was now near it, still cautiously creeping. The first danger to which he was exposed was this; that his enemy within the recess might push him down from the rocks with a touch. But on the other hand, there were three or four men ready to fire, the moment that a hand should be put forth; and then Morton could swim,—was known to be a strong swimmer;—whereas of Aaron Trow it was already declared by the prison gaolers that he could not swim. Two of the warders had now followed Morton on the rocks, so that in the event of his making good his entrance into the cavern, and holding his enemy at bay for a minute, he would be joined by aid.

It was strange to see how those different men conducted themselves as they stood on the opposite platform watching the attack. The officers from the prison had no other thought but of their prisoner, and were intent on taking him alive or dead. To them it was little or nothing what became of Morton. It was their business to encounter peril, and they were ready to do so;—feeling, however, by no means sorry to have such a man as Morton in advance of them. Very little was said by them. They had their wits about them, and remembered that every word spoken for the guidance of their ally would be heard also by the escaped convict. Their prey was sure, sooner or later, and had not Morton been so eager in his pursuit, they would have waited till some plan had been devised of trapping him without danger. But the townsmen from St. George, of whom some dozen were now standing there, were quick and eager and loud in their counsels. "Stay where you are, Mr. Morton,—stay awhile for the love of God—or he'll have you down." "Now's your time, Caleb; in on him now, and you'll have him." "Close with him, Morton, close with him at once; it's your only chance." "There's four of us here; we'll fire on him if he as much as shows a limb." All of which words as they were heard by that poor wretch within, must have sounded to him as the barking of a pack of hounds thirsting for his blood. For him at any rate there was no longer any hope in this world.

My reader, when chance has taken you into the hunting-field, has it ever been your lot to sit by on horseback, and watch the digging out of a fox? The operation is not an uncommon one, and in some countries it is held to be in accordance with the rules of fair sport. For myself, I think that when the brute has so far saved himself, he should be entitled to the benefit of his cunning; but I will not now discuss the propriety or impropriety of that practice in venery. I can never, however, watch the doing of that work without thinking much of the agonising struggles of the poor beast whose last refuge is being torn from over his head. There he lies within a few yards of his arch enemy, the huntsman. The thick breath of the hounds make hot the air within his hole. The sound of their voices is close upon his ears. His breast is nearly bursting with the violence of that effort which at last has brought him to his retreat. And then pickaxe and mattock are plied above his head, and nearer and more near to him press his foes,—his double foes, human and canine,—till at last a huge hand grasps him, and he is dragged forth among his enemies. Almost as soon as his eyes have seen the light the eager noses of a dozen hounds have moistened themselves in his entrails. Ah me! I know that he is vermin, the vermin after whom I have been risking my neck, with a bold ambition that I might ultimately witness his death-struggles; but, nevertheless, I would fain have saved him that last half hour of gradually diminished hope.

And Aaron Trow was now like a hunted fox, doomed to be dug out from his last refuge, with this addition to his misery, that these hounds when they caught their prey, would not put him at once out of his misery. When first he saw that throng of men coming down from the hill top and resting on the platform; he knew that his fate was come. When they called to him to surrender himself he was silent, but he knew that his silence was of no avail. To them who were so eager to be his captors the matter seemed to be still one of considerable difficulty; but, to his thinking, there was no difficulty. There were there some score of men, fully armed, within twenty yards of him. If he but showed a trace of his limbs he would become a mark for their bullets. And then if he were wounded, and no one would come to him! If they allowed him to lie there without food till he perished! Would it not be well for him to yield himself? Then they called again and he was still silent. That idea of yielding is very terrible to the heart of a man. And when the worst had come to the worst, did not the ocean run deep beneath his cavern's month?

But as they yelled at him and hallooed, making their preparations for his death, his presence of mind deserted the poor wretch. He had stolen an old pistol on one of his marauding expeditions, of which one barrel had been loaded. That in his mad despair he had fired; and now, as he lay near the mouth of the cavern, under the cover of the projecting stone, he had no weapon with him but his hands. He had had a knife, but that had dropped from him during the struggle on the floor of the cottage. He had now nothing but his hands, and was considering how he might best use them in ridding himself of the first of his pursuers. The man was near him, armed, with all the power and majesty of right on his side; whereas on his side, Aaron Trow had nothing,—not a hope. He raised his head that he might look forth, and a dozen voices shouted as his face appeared above the aperture. A dozen weapons were levelled at him, and he could see the gleaming of the muzzles of the guns. And then the foot of his pursuer was already on the corner stone at the cavern's mouth. "Now, Caleb, on him at once!" shouted a voice. Ah me! it was a moment in which to pity even such a man as Aaron Trow.

"Now, Caleb, at him at once!" shouted the voice. No, by heavens; not so, even yet! The sound of triumph in those words raised the last burst of energy in the breast of that wretched man; and he sprang forth, head foremost, from his prison house. Forth he came, manifest enough before the eyes of them all, and with head well down, and hands outstretched, but with his wide glaring eyes still turned towards his pursuers as he fell, he plunged down into the waves beneath him. Two of those who stood by, almost unconscious of what they did, fired at his body as it made its rapid way to the water; but, as they afterwards found, neither of the bullets struck him. Morton, when his prey thus leaped forth, escaping him for awhile, was already on the verge of the cavern,—had even then prepared his foot for that onward spring which should bring him to the throat of his foe. But he arrested himself, and for a moment stood there watching the body as it struck the water, and hid itself at once beneath the ripple. He stood there for a moment watching the deed and its effect, and then leaving his hold upon the rock, he once again followed his quarry. Down he went, head foremost, right on to the track in the waves which the other had made; and when the two rose to the surface together, each was struggling in the grasp of the other.

It was a foolish, nay, a mad deed to do. The poor wretch who had first fallen could not have escaped. He could not even swim, and had therefore flung himself to certain destruction when he took that leap from out of the cavern's mouth. It would have been sad to see him perish beneath the waves,—to watch him as he rose, gasping for breath, and then to see to him sinking again, to rise again, and then to go for ever. But his life had been fairly forfeit,—and why should one so much more precious have been flung after it? It was surely with no view of saving that pitiful life that Caleb Morton had leaped after his enemy. But the hound, hot with the chase, will follow the stag over the precipice and dash himself to pieces against the rocks. The beast thirsting for blood will rush in even among the weapons of men. Morton in his fury had felt but one desire, burned with but one passion. If the Fates would but grant him to fix his clutches in the throat of the man who had ill-used his love; for the rest it might all go as it would.

In the earlier part of the morning, while they were all searching for their victim, they had brought a boat up into this very inlet among the rocks; and the same boat had been at hand during the whole day. Unluckily, before they had come hither, it had been taken round the headland to a place among the rocks at which a government skiff is always moored. The sea was still so quiet that there was hardly a ripple on it, and the boat had been again sent for when first it was supposed that they had at last traced Aaron Trow to his hiding-place. Anxiously now were all eyes turned to the headland, but as yet no boat was there.

The two men rose to the surface, each struggling in the arms of the other. Trow, though he was in an element to which he was not used, though he had sprung thither as another suicide might spring to certain death beneath a railway engine, did not altogether lose his presence of mind. Prompted by a double instinct, he had clutched hold of Morton's body when he encountered it beneath the waters. He held on to it, as to his only protection, and he held on to him also as to his only enemy. If there was a chance for a life struggle, they would share that chance together; and if not, then together would they meet that other fate.

Caleb Morton was a very strong man, and though one of his arms was altogether encumbered by his antagonist, his other arm and his legs were free. With these he seemed to succeed in keeping his head above the water, weighted as he was with the body of his foe. But Trow's efforts were also used with the view of keeping himself above the water. Though he had purposed to destroy himself in taking that leap, and now hoped for nothing better than that they might both perish together, he yet struggled to keep his head above the waves. Bodily power he had none left to him, except that of holding on to Morton's arm and plunging with his legs; but he did hold on, and thus both their heads remained above the surface.

But this could not last long. It was easy to see that Trow's strength was nearly spent, and that when he went down Morton must go with him. If indeed they could be separated,—if Morton could once make himself free from that embrace into which he had been so anxious to leap,—then indeed there might be a hope. All round that little inlet the rock fell sheer down into the deep sea, so that there was no resting-place for a foot; it but round the headlands on either side, even within forty or fifty yards of that spot, Morton might rest on the rocks, till a boat should come to his assistance. To him that distance would have been nothing, if only his limbs had been at liberty.

Upon the platform of rocks they were all at their wits' ends. Many were anxious to fire at Trow; but even if they hit him, would Morton's position have been better? Would not the wounded man have still clung to him who was not wounded? And then there could be no certainty that any one of them would hit the right man. The ripple of the waves, though it was very slight, nevertheless sufficed to keep the bodies in motion; and then, too, there was not among them any marksman peculiar for his skill.

Morton's efforts in the water were too severe to admit of his speaking, but he could hear and understand the words which were addressed to him. "Shake him off, Caleb." "Strike him from you with your foot." "Swim to the right shore; swim for it, even if you take him with you." Yes; he could hear them all; but hearing and obeying were very different. It was not easy to shake off that dying man; and as for swimming with him, that was clearly impossible. It was as much as he could do to keep his head above water, let alone any attempt to move in one settled direction.

For some four or five minutes they lay thus battling on the waves before the head of either of them went down. Trow had been twice below the surface, but it was before he had succeeded in supporting himself by Morton's arm. Now it seemed as though he must sink again,—as though both must sink. His mouth was barely kept above the water, and as Morton shook him with his arm, the tide would pass over him. It was horrid to watch from the shore the glaring upturned eyes of the dying wretch, as his long streaming hair lay back upon the wave. "Now, Caleb, hold him down. Hold him under," was shouted in the voice of some eager friend. Rising up on the water, Morton made a last effort to do as he was bid. He did press the man's head down,—well down below the surface,—but still the hand clung to him, and as he struck out against the water, he was powerless against that grasp.

Then there came a loud shout along the shore, and all those on the platform, whose eyes had been fixed so closely on that terrible struggle beneath them, rushed towards the rocks on the other coast. The sound of oars was heard close to them,—an eager pressing stroke, as of men who knew well that they were rowing for the salvation of a life. On they came, close under the rocks, obeying with every muscle of their bodies the behests of those who called to them from the shore. The boat came with such rapidity,—was so recklessly urged, that it was driven somewhat beyond the inlet; but in passing, a blow was struck which made Caleb Morton once more the master of his own life. The two men had been carried out in their struggle towards the open sea; and as the boat curved in, so as to be as close as the rocks would allow, the bodies of the men were brought within the sweep of the oars. He in the bow—for there were four pulling in the boat—had raised his oar as he neared the rocks,—had raised it high above the water; and now, as they passed close by the struggling men, he let it fall with all its force on the upturned face of the wretched convict. It was a terrible, frightful thing to do,—thus striking one who was so stricken; but who shall say that the blow was not good and just? Methinks, however, that the eyes and face of that dying man will haunt for ever the dreams of him who carried that oar!

Trow never rose again to the surface. Three days afterwards his body was found at the ferry, and then they carried him to the convict island and buried him. Morton was picked up and taken into the boat. His life was saved; but it may be a question how the battle might have gone had not that friendly oar been raised in his behalf. As it was, he lay at the cottage for days before he was able to be moved, so as to receive the congratulations of those who had watched that terrible conflict from the shore. Nor did he feel that there had been anything in that day's work of which he could be proud;— much rather of which it behoved him to be thoroughly ashamed. Some six months after that he obtained the hand of Anastasia Bergen, but they did not remain long in Bermuda. "He went away, back to his own country," my informant told me; "because he could not endure to meet the ghost of Aaron Trow, at that point of the road which passes near the cottage." That the ghost of Aaron Trow may be seen there and round the little rocky inlet of the sea, is part of the creed of every young woman in Bermuda.

The Chateau of
Prince Polignac

The Chateau of
Prince Polignac

FEW ENGLISHMEN OR ENGLISHWOMEN are intimately acquainted with the little town of Le Puy. It is the capital of the old province of Le Velay, which also is now but little known, even to French ears, for it is in these days called by the imperial name of the Department of the Haute Loire. It is to the south-east of Auvergne, and is nearly in the centre of the southern half of France.

But few towns, merely as towns, can be better worth visiting. In the first place, the volcanic formation of the ground on which it stands is not only singular in the extreme, so as to be interesting to the geologist, but it is so picturesque as to be equally gratifying to the general tourist. Within a narrow valley there stand several rocks, rising up from the ground with absolute abruptness. Round two of these the town clusters, and a third stands but a mile distant, forming the centre of a faubourg, or suburb. These rocks appear to be, and I believe are, the harder particles of volcanic matter, which have not been carried away through successive ages by the joint agency of water and air.

When the tide of lava ran down between the hills the surface left was no doubt on a level with the heads of these rocks; but here and there the deposit became harder than elsewhere, and these harder points have remained, lifting up their steep heads in a line through the valley.

The highest of these is called the Rocher de Corneille. Round this and up its steep sides the town stands. On its highest summit there was an old castle; and there now is, or will be before these pages are printed, a co-lossal figure in bronze of the Virgin Mary, made from the cannon taken at Sebastopol. Half-way down the hill the cathedral is built, a singularly gloomy edifice,— Romanesque, as it is called, in its style, but extremely similar in its mode of architecture to what we know of Byzantine structures. But there has been no surface on the rock side large enough to form a resting-place for the church, which has therefore been built out on huge supporting piles, which form a porch below the west front; so that the approach is by numerous steps laid along the side of the wall below the church, forming a wondrous flight of stairs. Let all men who may find themselves stopping at Le Puy visit the top of these stairs at the time of the setting sun, and look down from thence through the framework of the porch on the town beneath, and at the hill-side beyond.

Behind the church is the seminary of the priests, with its beautiful walks stretching round the Rocher de Cor-neille, and overlooking the town and valley below.

Next to this rock, and within a quarter of a mile of it, is the second peak, called the Rock of the Needle. It rises narrow, sharp, and abrupt from the valley, allowing of no buildings on its sides. But on its very point has been erected a church sacred to St. Michael, that lover of rock summits, accessible by stairs cut from the stone. This, perhaps—this rock, I mean—is the most wonderful of the wonders which Nature has formed at La Puy.

Above this, at a mile's distance, is the rock of Espailly, formed in the same way, and almost equally precipitous. On its summit is a castle, having its own legend, and professing to have been the residence of Charles VII., when little of France belonged to its kings but the provinces of Berry, Auvergne, and Le Velay. Some three miles farther up there is another volcanic rock, larger, indeed, but equally sudden in its spring,—equally remarkable as rising abruptly from the valley,—on which stands the castle and old family residence of the house of Polignac. It was lost by them at the Revolution, but was repurchased by the minister of Charles X., and is still the property of the head of the race.

Le Puy itself is a small, moderate, pleasant French town, in which the language of the people has not the pure Parisian aroma, nor is the glory of the boulevards of the capital emulated in its streets. These are crooked, narrow, steep, and intricate, forming here and there excellent sketches for a lover of street picturesque beauty; but hurtful to the feet with their small, round-topped paving stones, and not always as clean as pedestrian ladies might desire.

And now I would ask my readers to join me at the morning table d'hote at the Hotel des Ambassadeurs. It will of course be understood that this does not mean a breakfast in the ordinary fashion of England, consisting of tea or coffee, bread and butter, and perhaps a boiled egg. It comprises all the requisites for a composite dinner, excepting soup; and as one gets farther south in France, this meal is called dinner. It is, however, eaten without any prejudice to another similar and somewhat longer meal at six or seven o'clock, which, when the above name is taken up by the earlier enterprise, is styled supper.

The dejeuner, or dinner, at the Hotel des Ambassadeurs, on the morning in question, though very elaborate, was not a very gay affair. There were some fourteen persons present, of whom half were residents in the town, men employed in some official capacity, who found this to be the cheapest, the most luxurious, and to them the most comfortable mode of living. They clustered together at the head of the table, and as they were customary guests at the house, they talked their little talk together—it was very little—and made the most of the good things before them. Then there were two or three commis-voyageurs, a chance traveller or two, and an English lady with a young daughter. The English lady sat next to one of the accustomed guests; but he, unlike the others, held converse with her rather than with them. Our story at present has reference only to that lady and to that gentleman.

Place aux dames. We will speak first of the lady, whose name was Mrs. Thompson. She was, shall I say, a young woman of about thirty-six. In so saying, I am perhaps creating a prejudice against her in the minds of some readers, as they will, not unnaturally, suppose her, after such an announcement, to be in truth over forty. Any such prejudice will be unjust. I would have it believed that thirty-six was the outside, not the inside of her age. She was good-looking, lady-like, and considering that she was an Englishwoman, fairly well dressed. She was inclined to be rather full in her person, but perhaps not more so than is becoming to ladies at her time of life. She had rings on her fingers and a brooch on her bosom which were of some value, and on the back of her head she wore a jaunty small lace cap, which seemed to tell, in conjunction with her other appointments, that her circumstances were comfortable.

The little girl who sat next to her was the youngest of her two daughters, and might be about thirteen years of age. Her name was Matilda, but infantine circumstances had invested her with the nickname of Mimmy, by which her mother always called her. A nice, pretty, playful little girl was Mimmy Thompson, wearing two long tails of plaited hair hanging, behind her head, and inclined occasionally to be rather loud in her sport.

Mrs. Thompson had another and an elder daughter, now some fifteen years old, who was at school in Le Puy; and it was with reference to her tuition that Mrs. Thompson had taken up a temporary residence at the Hotel des Ambassadeurs in that town. Lilian Thompson was occasionally invited down to dine or breakfast at the inn, and was visited daily at her school by her mother.

"When I'm sure that she'll do, I shall leave her there, and go back to England," Mrs. Thompson had said, not in the purest French, to the neighbour who always sat next to her at the table d'hote, the gentleman, namely, to whom we have above alluded. But still she had remained at Le Puy a month, and did not go; a circumstance which was considered singular, but by no means unpleasant, both by the innkeeper and by the gentleman in question.

The facts, as regarded Mrs. Thompson, were as follows:- She was the widow of a gentleman who had served for many years in the civil service of the East Indies, and who, on dying, had left her a comfortable income of—it matters not how many pounds, but constituting quite a sufficiency to enable her to live at her ease and educate her daughters.

Her children had been sent home to England before her husband's death, and after that event she had followed them; but there, though she was possessed of moderate wealth, she had no friends and few acquaintances, and after a little while she had found life to be rather dull. Her customs were not those of England, nor were her propensities English; therefore she had gone abroad, and having received some recommendation of this school at Le Puy, had made her way thither. As it appeared to her that she really enjoyed more consideration at Le Puy than had been accorded to her either at Torquay or Leamington, there she remained from day to day. The total payment required at the Hotel des Ambassadeurs was but six francs daily for herself and three and a half for her little girl; and where else could she live with a better junction of economy and comfort? And then the gentleman who always sat next to her was so exceedingly civil!

The gentleman's name was M. Lacordaire. So much she knew, and had learned to call him by his name very frequently. Mimmy, too, was quite intimate with M. Lacordaire; but nothing more than his name was known of him. But M. Lacordaire carried a general letter of recommendation in his face, manner, gait, dress, and tone of voice. In all these respects there was nothing left to be desired; and, in addition to this, he was decorated, and wore the little red ribbon of the Legion of Honour, ingeniously twisted into the shape of a small flower.

M. Lacordaire might be senior in age to Mrs. Thompson by about ten years, nor had he about him any of the airs or graces of a would-be young man. His hair, which he wore very short, was grizzled, as was also the small pretence of a whisker which came down about as far as the middle of his ear; but the tuft on his chin was still brown, without a gray hair. His eyes were bright and tender, his voice was low and soft, his hands were very white, his clothes were always new and well fitting, and a better-brushed hat could not be seen out of Paris, nor perhaps in it.

Now, during the weeks which Mrs. Thompson had passed at La Puy, the acquaintance which she had formed with M. Lacordaire had progressed beyond the prolonged meals in the salle a manger. He had occasionally sat beside her evening table as she took her English cup of tea in her own room, her bed being duly screened off in its distant niche by becoming curtains; and then he had occasionally walked beside her, as he civilly escorted her to the lions of the place; and he had once accompanied her, sitting on the back seat of a French voiture, when she had gone forth to see something of the surrounding country.

On all such occasions she had been accompanied by one of her daughters, and the world of Le Puy had had nothing material to say against her. But still the world of Le Puy had whispered a little, suggesting that M. Lacordaire knew very well what he was about. But might not Mrs. Thompson also know as well what she was about? At any rate, everything had gone on very pleasantly since the acquaintance had been made. And now, so much having been explained, we will go back to the elaborate breakfast at the Hotel des Ambassadeurs.

Mrs. Thompson, holding Mimmy by the hand, walked into the room some few minutes after the last bell had been rung, and took the place which was now hers by custom. The gentlemen who constantly frequented the house all bowed to her, but M. Lacordaire rose from his seat and offered her his hand.

"And how is Mees Meemy this morning?" said he; for 'twas thus he always pronounced her name.

Miss Mimmy, answering for herself, declared that she was very well, and suggested that M. Lacordaire should give her a fig from off a dish that was placed immediately before him on the table. This M. Lacordaire did, presenting it very elegantly between his two fingers, and making a little bow to the little lady as he did so.

"Fie, Mimmy!" said her mother; "why do you ask for the things before the waiter brings them round?"

"But, mamma," said Mimmy, speaking English, "M. Lacordaire always gives me a fig every morning."

"M. Lacordaire always spoils you, I think," answered Mrs. Thompson, in French. And then they went thoroughly to work at their breakfast. During the whole meal M. Lacordaire attended assiduously to his neighbour; and did so without any evil result, except that one Frenchman with a black moustache, at the head of the table, trod on the toe of another Frenchman with another black moustache—winking as he made the sign—just as M. Lacordaire, having selected a bunch of grapes, put it on Mrs. Thompson's plate with infinite grace. But who among us all is free from such impertinences as these?

"But madame really must see the chateau of Prince Polignac before she leaves Le Puy," said M. Lacordaire.

"The chateau of who?" asked Mimmy, to whose young ears the French words were already becoming familiar.

"Prince Polignac, my dear. Well, I really don't know, M. Lacordaire;—I have seen a great deal of the place already, and I shall be going now very soon; probably in a day or two," said Mrs. Thompson.

"But madame must positively see the chateau," said M. Lacordaire, very impressively; and then after a pause he added, "If madame will have the complaisance to commission me to procure a carriage for this afternoon, and will allow me the honour to be her guide, I shall consider myself one of the most fortunate of men."

"Oh, yes, mamma, do go," said Mimmy, clapping her hands. "And it is Thursday, and Lilian can go with us."

"Be quiet, Mimmy, do. Thank you, no, M. Lacordaire. I could not go to-day; but I am extremely obliged by your politeness."

M. Lacordaire still pressed the matter, and Mrs. Thompson still declined till it was time to rise from the table. She then declared that she did not think it possible that she should visit the chateau before she left Le Puy; but that she would give him an answer at dinner.

The most tedious time in the day to Mrs. Thompson were the two hours after breakfast. At one o'clock she daily went to the school, taking Mimmy, who for an hour or two shared her sister's lessons. This and her little excursions about the place, and her shopping, managed to make away with her afternoon. Then in the evening, she generally saw something of M. Lacordaire. But those two hours after breakfast were hard of killing.

On this occasion, when she gained her own room, she as usual placed Mimmy on the sofa with a needle. Her custom then was to take up a novel; but on this morning she sat herself down in her arm-chair, and resting her head upon her hand and elbow, began to turn over certain circumstances in her mind.

"Mamma," said Mimmy, "why won't you go with M. Lacordaire to that place belonging to the prince? Prince—Polly something, wasn't it?"

"Mind your work, my dear," said Mrs. Thompson.

"But I do so wish you'd go, mamma. What was the prince's name?"

"Polignac."

"Mamma, ain't princes very great people?"

"Yes, my dear; sometimes."

"Is Prince Polly-nac like our Prince Alfred?"

"No, my dear; not at all. At least, I suppose not."

"Is his mother a queen?"

"No, my dear."

"Then his father must be a king?"

"No, my dear. It is quite a different thing here. Here in France they have a great many princes."

"Well, at any rate I should like to see a prince's chateau; so I do hope you'll go." And then there was a pause. "Mamma, could it come to pass, here in France, that M. Lacordaire should ever be a prince?"

"M. Lacordaire a prince! No; don't talk such nonsense, but mind your work."

"Isn't M. Lacordaire a very nice man? Ain't you very fond of him?"

To this question Mrs. Thompson made no answer.

"Mamma," continued Mimmy, after a moment's pause, "won't you tell me whether you are fond of M. Lacordaire? I'm quite sure of this,—that he's very fond of you."

"What makes you think that?" asked Mrs. Thompson, who could not bring herself to refrain from the question.

"Because he looks at you in that way, mamma, and squeezes your hand."

"Nonsense, child," said Mrs. Thompson; "hold your tongue. I don't know what can have put such stuff into your head."

"But he does, mamma," said Mimmy, who rarely allowed her mother to put her down.

Mrs. Thompson made no further answer, but again sat with her head resting on her hand. She also, if the truth must be told, was thinking of M. Lacordaire and his fondness for herself. He had squeezed her hand and he had looked into her face. However much it may have been nonsense on Mimmy's part to talk of such things, they had not the less absolutely occurred. Was it really the fact that M. Lacordaire was in love with her?

And if so, what return should she, or could she make to such a passion? He had looked at her yesterday, and squeezed her hand to-day. Might it not be probable that he would advance a step further to-morrow? If so, what answer would she be prepared to make to him?

She did not think—so she said to herself—that she had any particular objection to marrying again. Thompson had been dead now for four years, and neither his friends, nor her friends, nor the world could say she was wrong on that score. And as to marrying a Frenchman, she could not say she felt within herself any absolute repugnance to doing that. Of her own country, speaking of England as such, she, in truth, knew but little— and perhaps cared less. She had gone to India almost as a child, and England had not been specially kind to her on her return. She had found it dull and cold, stiff, and almost ill-natured. People there had not smiled on her and been civil as M. Lacordaire had done. As far as England and Englishmen were considered she saw no reason why she should not marry M. Lacordaire.

And then, as regarded the man; could she in her heart say that she was prepared to love, honour, and obey M. Lacordaire? She certainly knew no reason why she should not do so. She did not know much of him, she said to herself at first; but she knew as much, she said afterwards, as she had known personally of Mr. Thompson before their marriage. She had known, to be sure, what was Mr. Thompson's profession and what his income; or, if not, some one else had known for her. As to both these points she was quite in the dark as regarded M. Lacordaire.

Personally, she certainly did like him, as she said to herself more than once. There was a courtesy and soft-ness about him which were very gratifying to her; and then, his appearance was so much in his favour. He was not very young, she acknowledged; but neither was she young herself. It was quite evident that he was fond of her children, and that he would be a kind and affec-tionate father to them. Indeed, there was kindness in all that he did.

Should she marry again,—and she put it to herself quite hypothetically,—she would look for no romance in such a second marriage. She would be content to sit down in a quiet home, to the tame dull realities of life, satisfied with the companionship of a man who would be kind and gentle to her, and whom she could respect and esteem. Where could she find a companion with whom this could be more safely anticipated than with M. Lacordaire?

And so she argued the question within her own breast in a manner not unfriendly to that gentleman. That there was as yet one great hindrance she at once saw; but then that might be remedied by a word. She did not know what was his income or his profession. The chambermaid, whom she had interrogated, had told her that he was a "marchand." To merchants, generally, she felt that she had no objection. The Barings and the Rothschilds were merchants, as was also that wonderful man at Bombay, Sir Hommajee Bommajee, who was worth she did no know how many thousand lacs of rupees.

That it would behove her, on her own account and that of her daughters, to take care of her own little fortune in contracting any such connection, that she felt strongly. She would never so commit herself as to put security in that respect out of her power. But then she did not think that M. Lacordaire would ever ask her to do so; at any rate, she was determined on this, that there should never be any doubt on that matter; and as she firmly resolved on this, she again took up her book, and for a minute or two made an attempt to read.

"Mamma," said Mummy, "will M. Lacordaire go up to the school to see Lilian when you go away from this?"

"Indeed, I cannot say, my dear. If Lilian is a good girl, perhaps he may do so now and then."

"And will he write to you and tell you how she is?"

"Lilian can write for herself; can she not?"

"Oh yes; I suppose she can; but I hope M. Lacordaire will write too. We shall come back here some day; shan't we, mamma?"

"I cannot say, my dear."

"I do so hope we shall see M. Lacordaire again. Do you know what I was thinking, mamma?"

"Little girls like you ought not to think," said Mrs. Thompson, walking slowly out of the room to the top of the stairs and back again; for she had felt the necessity of preventing Mimmy from disclosing any more of her thoughts. "And now, my dear, get yourself ready, and we will go up to the school."

Mrs. Thompson always dressed herself with care, though not in especially fine clothes, before she went down to dinner at the table d'hote; but on this occasion she was more than usually particular. She hardly explained to herself why she did this; but, nevertheless, as she stood before the glass, she did in a certain manner feel that the circumstances of her future life might perhaps depend on what might be said and done that evening. She had not absolutely decided whether or no she would go to the Prince's chateau; but if she did go -. Well, if she did; what then? She had sense enough, as she assured herself more than once, to regulate her own conduct with propriety in any such emergency.

During the dinner, M. Lacordaire conversed in his usual manner, but said nothing whatever about the visit to Polignac. He was very kind to Mimmy, and very courteous to her mother, but did not appear to be at all more particular than usual. Indeed, it might be a question whether he was not less so. As she had entered the room Mrs. Thompson had said to herself that, perhaps, after all, it would be better that there should be nothing more thought about it; but before the four of five courses were over, she was beginning to feel a little disappointed.

And now the fruit was on the table, after the consumption of which it was her practice to retire. It was certainly open to her to ask M. Lacordaire to take tea with her that evening, as she had done on former occasions; but she felt that she must not do this now, considering the immediate circumstances of the case. If any further steps were to be taken, they must be taken by him, and not by her;—or else by Mimmy, who, just as her mother was slowly consuming her last grapes, ran round to the back of M. Lacordaire's chair, and whispered something into his ear. It may be presumed that Mrs. Thompson did not see the intention of the movement in time to arrest it, for she did nothing till the whispering had been whispered; and then she rebuked the child, bade her not to be troublesome, and with more than usual austerity in her voice, desired her to get herself ready to go up stairs to their chamber.

As she spoke she herself rose from her chair, and made her final little bow to the table, and her other final little bow and smile to M. Lacordaire; but this was certain to all who saw it, that the smile was not as gracious as usual.

As she walked forth, M. Lacordaire rose from his chair—such being his constant practice when she left the table; but on this occasion he accompanied her to the door.

"And has madame decided," he asked, "whether she will permit me to accompany her to the chateau?"

"Well, I really don't know," said Mrs. Thompson.

"Mees Meemy," continued M. Lacordaire, "is very anxious to see the rock, and I may perhaps hope that Mees Lilian would be pleased with such a little excursion. As for myself—" and then M. Lacordaire put his hand upon his heart in a manner that seemed to speak more plainly than he had ever spoken.

"Well, if the children would really like it, and—as you are so very kind," said Mrs. Thompson; and so the matter was conceded.

"To-morrow afternoon?" suggested M. Lacordaire. But Mrs. Thompson fixed on Saturday, thereby showing that she herself was in no hurry for the expedition.

"Oh, I am so glad!" said Mimmy, when they had re-entered their own room. "Mamma, do let me tell Lilian myself when I go up to the school to-morrow!"

But mamma was in no humour to say much to her child on this subject at the present moment. She threw herself back on her sofa in perfect silence, and began to reflect whether she would like to sign her name in future as Fanny Lacordaire, instead of Fanny Thompson. It certainly seemed as though things were verging towards such a necessity. A marchand! But a marchand of what? She had an instinctive feeling that the people in the hotel were talking about her and M. Lacordaire, and was therefore more than ever averse to asking any one a question.

As she went up to the school the next afternoon, she walked through more of the streets of Le Puy than was necessary, and in every street she looked at the names which she saw over the doors of the more respectable houses of business. But she looked in vain. It might be that M. Lacordaire was a marchand of so specially high a quality as to be under no necessity to put up his name at all. Sir Hommajee Bommajee's name did not appear over any door in Bombay;—at least, she thought not.

And then came the Saturday morning. "We shall be ready at two," she said, as she left the breakfast-table; "and perhaps you would not mind calling for Lilian on the way."

M. Lacordaire would be delighted to call anywhere for anybody on behalf of Mrs. Thompson; and then, as he got to the door of the salon, he offered her his hand. He did so with so much French courtesy that she could not refuse it, and then she felt that his purpose was more tender than ever it had been. And why not, if this was the destiny which Fate had prepared for her?

Mrs. Thompson would rather have got into the carriage at any other spot in Le Puy than at that at which she was forced to do so—the chief entrance, namely, of the Hotel des Ambassadeurs. And what made it worse was this, that an appearance of a special fate was given to the occasion. M. Lacordaire was dressed in more than his Sunday best. He had on new yellow kid gloves. His coat, if not new, was newer than any Mrs. Thompson had yet observed, and was lined with silk up to the very collar. He had on patent leather boots, which glittered, as Mrs. Thompson thought, much too conspicuously. And as for his hat, it was quite evident that it was fresh that morning from the maker's block.

In this costume, with his hat in his hand, he stood under the great gateway of the hotel, ready to hand Mrs. Thompson into the carriage. This would have been nothing if the landlord and landlady had not been there also, as well as the man-cook, and the four waiters, and the fille de chambre. Two or three other pair of eyes Mrs. Thompson also saw, as she glanced round, and then Mimmy walked across the yard in her best clothes with a fete-day air about her for which her mother would have liked to have whipped her.

But what did it matter? If it was written in the book that she should become Madame Lacordaire, of course the world would know that there must have been some preparatory love-making. Let them have their laugh;

a good husband would not be dearly purchased at so trifling an expense. And so they sallied forth with already half the ceremony of a wedding.

Mimmy seated herself opposite to her mother, and M. Lacordaire also sat with his back to the horses, leaving the second place of honour for Lilian. "Pray make yourself comfortable, M. Lacordaire, and don't mind her," said Mrs. Thompson. But he was firm in his purpose of civility, perhaps making up his mind that when he should in truth stand in the place of papa to the young lady, then would be his time for having the back seat in the carnage.

Lilian, also in her best frock, came down the schoolsteps, and three of the school teachers came with her. It would have added to Mrs. Thompson's happiness at that moment if M. Lacordaire would have kept his polished boots out of sight, and put his yellow gloves into his pocket.

And then they started. The road from Le Puy to Polignac is nearly all up hill; and a very steep hill it is, so that there was plenty of time for conversation. But the girls had it nearly all to themselves. Mimmy thought that she had never found M. Lacordaire so stupid; and Lilian told her sister on the first safe opportunity that occurred, that it seemed very much as though they were all going to church.

"And do any of the Polignac people ever live at this place?" asked Mrs. Thompson, by way of making conversation; in answer to which M. Lacordaire informed madame that the place was at present only a ruin; and then there was again silence till they found themselves under the rock, and were informed by the driver that the rest of the ascent must be made on foot.

The rock now stood abrupt and precipitous above their heads. It was larger in its circumference and with much larger space on its summit than those other volcanic rocks in and close to the town; but then at the same time it was higher from the ground, and quite as inaccessible, except by the single path which led up to the chateau.

M. Lacordaire, with conspicuous gallantry, first assisted Mrs. Thompson from the carriage, and then handed down the two young ladies. No lady could have been so difficult to please as to complain of him, and yet Mrs. Thompson thought that he was not as agreeable as usual. Those horrid boots and those horrid gloves gave him such an air of holiday finery that neither could he be at his ease wearing them, nor could she, in seeing them worn.

They were soon taken in hand by the poor woman whose privilege it was to show the ruins. For a little distance they walked up the path in single file; not that it was too narrow to accommodate two, but M. Lacordaire's courage had not yet been screwed to a point which admitted of his offering his arm to the widow. For in France, it must be remembered, that this means more than it does in some other countries.

Mrs. Thompson felt that all this was silly and useless. If they were not to be dear friends this coming out feting together, those boots and gloves and new hat were all very foolish; and if they were, the sooner they understood each other the better. So Mrs. Thompson, finding that the path was steep and the weather warm, stood still for a while leaning against the wall, with a look of considerable fatigue in her face.

"Will madame permit me the honour of offering her my arm?" said M. Lacordaire. "The road is so extraordinarily steep for madame to climb."

Mrs. Thompson did permit him the honour, and so they went on till they reached the top.

The view from the summit was both extensive and grand, but neither Lilian nor Mimmy were much pleased with the place. The elder sister, who had talked over the matter with her school companions, expected a fine castle with turrets, battlements, and romance; and the other expected a pretty smiling house, such as princes, in her mind, ought to inhabit.

Instead of this they found an old turret, with steps so broken that M. Lacordaire did not care to ascend them, and the ruined walls of a mansion, in which nothing was to be seen but the remains of an enormous kitchen chimney.

"It was the kitchen of the family," said the guide.

"Oh," said Mrs. Thompson.

"And this," said the woman, taking them into the next ruined compartment, "was the kitchen of monsieur et madame."

"What! two kitchens?" exclaimed Lilian, upon which M. Lacordaire explained that the ancestors of the Prince de Polignac had been very great people, and had therefore required culinary performances on a great scale.

And then the woman began to chatter something about an oracle of Apollo. There was, she said, a hole in the rock, from which in past times, perhaps more than a hundred years ago, the oracle used to speak forth mysterious words.

"There," she said, pointing to a part of the rock at some distance, "was the hole. And if the ladies would follow her to a little outhouse which was just beyond, she would show them the huge stone mouth out of which the oracle used to speak."

Lilian and Mimmy both declared at once for seeing the oracle, but Mrs. Thompson expressed her determination to remain sitting where she was upon the turf. So the guide started off with the young ladies; and will it be thought surprising that M. Lacordaire should have remained alone by the side of Mrs. Thompson?

It must be now or never, Mrs. Thompson felt; and as regarded M. Lacordaire, he probably entertained some idea of the same kind. Mrs. Thompson's inclinations, though they had never been very strong in the matter, were certainly in favour of the "now." M. Lacordaire's inclinations were stronger. He had fully and firmly made up his mind in favour of matrimony; but then he was not so absolutely in favour of the "now." Mrs. Thompson's mind, if one could have read it, would have shown a great objection to shilly-shallying, as she was accustomed to call it. But M. Lacordaire, were it not for the danger which might thence arise, would have seen no objection to some slight further procrastination. His courage was beginning, perhaps, to ooze out from his fingers' ends.

"I declare that those girls have scampered away ever so far," said Mrs. Thompson.

"Would madame wish that I should call them back?" said M. Lacordaire, innocently.

"Oh, no, dear children! let them enjoy themselves; it will be a pleasure to them to run about the rock, and I suppose they will be safe with that woman?"

"Oh, yes, quite safe," said M. Lacordaire; and then there was another little pause.

Mrs. Thompson was sitting on a broken fragment of a stone just outside the entrance to the old family kitchen, and M. Lacordaire was standing immediately before her. He had in his hand a little cane with which he sometimes slapped his boots and sometimes poked about among the rubbish. His hat was not quite straight on his head, having a little jaunty twist to one side, with reference to which, by-the-bye, Mrs. Thompson then resolved that she would make a change, should ever the gentleman become her own property. He still wore his gloves, and was very smart; but it was clear to see that he was not at his ease.

"I hope the heat does not incommode you," he said after a few moments' silence. Mrs. Thompson declared that it did not, that she liked a good deal of heat, and that, on the whole, she was very well where she was. She was afraid, however, that she was detaining M. Lacordaire, who might probably wish to be moving about upon the rock. In answer to which M. Lacordaire declared that he never could be so happy anywhere as in her close vicinity.

"You are too good to me," said Mrs. Thompson, almost sighing. "I don't know what my stay here would have been without your great kindness."

"It is madame that has been kind to me," said M. Lacordaire, pressing the handle of his cane against his heart.

There was then another pause, after which Mrs. Thompson said that that was all his French politeness; that she knew that she had been very troublesome to him, but that she would now soon be gone; and that then, in her own country, she would never forget his great goodness.

"Ah, madame!" said M. Lacordaire; and, as he said it, much more was expressed in his face than in his words. But, then, you can neither accept nor reject a gentleman by what he says in his face. He blushed, too, up to his grizzled hair, and, turning round, walked a step or two away from the widow's seat, and back again.

Mrs. Thompson the while sat quite still. The displaced fragment, lying, as it did, near a corner of the building, made not an uncomfortable chair. She had only to be careful that she did not injure her hat or crush her clothes, and throw in a word here and there to assist the gentleman, should occasion permit it.

"Madame!" said M. Lacordaire, on his return from a second little walk.

"Monsieur!" replied Mrs. Thompson, perceiving that M. Lacordaire paused in his speech.

"Madame," he began again, and then, as he again paused, Mrs. Thompson looked up to him very sweetly; "madame, what I am going to say will, I am afraid, seem to evince by far too great audacity on my part."

Mrs. Thompson may, perhaps, have thought that, at the present moment, audacity was not his fault. She replied, however, that she was quite sure that monsieur would say nothing that was in any way unbecoming either for him to speak or for her to hear.

"Madame, may I have ground to hope that such may be your sentiments after I have spoken! Madame"—and now he went down, absolutely on his knees, on the hard stones; and Mrs. Thompson, looking about into the distance, almost thought that she saw the top of the guide's cap—"Madame, I have looked forward to this opportunity as one in which I may declare for you the greatest passion that I have ever yet felt. Madame, with all my heart and soul I love you. Madame, I offer to you the homage of my heart, my hand, the happiness of my life, and all that I possess in this world;" and then, taking her hand gracefully between his gloves, he pressed his lips against the tips of her fingers.

If the thing was to be done, this way of doing it was, perhaps, as good as any other. It was one, at any rate, which left no doubt whatever as to the gentleman's intentions. Mrs. Thompson, could she have had her own way, would not have allowed her lover of fifty to go down upon his knees, and would have spared him much of the romance of his declaration. So also would she have spared him his yellow gloves and his polished boots. But these were a part of the necessity of the situation, and therefore she wisely took them as matters to be passed over with indifference. Seeing, however, that M. Lacordaire still remained on his knees, it was necessary that she should take some step toward raising him, especially as her two children and the guide would infallibly be upon them before long.

"M. Lacordaire," she said, "you surprise me greatly; but pray get up."

"But will madame vouchsafe to give me some small ground for hope?"

"The girls will be here directly, M. Lacordaire; pray get up. I can talk to you much better if you will stand up, or sit down on one of these stones."

M. Lacordaire did as he was bid; he got up, wiped the knees of his pantaloons with his handkerchief, sat down beside her, and then pressed the handle of his cane to his heart.

"You really have so surprised me that I hardly know how to answer you," said Mrs. Thompson. "Indeed, I cannot bring myself to imagine that you are in earnest."

"Ah, madame, do not be so cruel! How can I have lived with you so long, sat beside you for so many days, without having received your image into my heart? I am in earnest! Alas! I fear too much in earnest!" And then he looked at her with all his eyes, and sighed with all his strength.

Mrs. Thompson's prudence told her that it would be well to settle the matter, in one way or the other, as soon as possible. Long periods of love-making were fit for younger people than herself and her future possible husband. Her object would be to make him comfortable if she could, and that he should do the same for her, if that also were possible. As for lookings and sighings and pressings of the hand, she had gone through all that some twenty years since in India, when Thompson had been young, and she was still in her teens.

"But, M. Lacordaire, there are so many things to be considered. There! I hear the children coming! Let us walk this way for a minute." And they turned behind a wall which placed them out of sight, and walked on a few paces till they reached a parapet, which stood on the uttermost edge of the high rock. Leaning upon this they continued their conversation.

"There are so many things to be considered," said Mrs. Thompson again.

"Yes, of course," said M. Lacordaire. "But my one great consideration is this;—that I love madame to distraction."

"I am very much flattered; of course, any lady would so feel. But, M. Lacordaire—"

"Madame, I am all attention. But, if you would deign to make me happy, say that one word, 'I love you!'" M. Lacordaire, as he uttered these words, did not look, as the saying is, at his best. But Mrs. Thompson forgave him. She knew that elderly gentlemen under such circumstances do not look at their best.

"But if I consented to—to—to such an arrangement, I could only do so on seeing that it would be beneficial—or, at any rate, not injurious—to my children; and that it would offer to ourselves a fair promise of future happiness."

"Ah, madame; it would be the dearest wish of my heart to be a second father to those two young ladies; except, indeed—" and then M. Lacordaire stopped the flow of his speech.

"In such matters it is so much the best to be explicit at once," said Mrs. Thompson.

"Oh, yes; certainly! Nothing can be more wise than madame."

"And the happiness of a household depends so much on money."

"Madame!"

"Let me say a word or two, Monsieur Lacordaire. I have enough for myself and my children; and, should I every marry again, I should not, I hope, be felt as a burden by my husband; but it would, of course, be my duty to know what were his circumstances before I accepted him. Of yourself, personally, I have seen nothing that I do not like."

"Oh, madame!"

"But as yet I know nothing of your circumstances."

M. Lacordaire, perhaps, did feel that Mrs. Thompson's prudence was of a strong, masculine description; but he hardly liked her the less on this account. To give him his due he was not desirous of marrying her solely for her money's sake. He also wished for a comfortable home, and proposed to give as much as he got; only he had been anxious to wrap up the solid cake of this business in a casing of sugar of romance. Mrs. Thompson would not have the sugar but the cake might not be the worse on that account.

"No, madame, not as yet; but they shall all be made open and at your disposal," said M. Lacordaire; and Mrs. Thompson bowed approvingly.

"I am in business," continued M. Lacordaire; "and my business gives me eight thousand francs a year."

"Four times eight are thirty-two," said Mrs. Thompson to herself; putting the francs into pounds sterling, in the manner that she had always found to be the readiest. Well, so far the statement was satisfactory. An income of three hundred and twenty pounds a year from business, joined to her own, might do very well. She did not in the least suspect M. Lacordaire of being false, and so far the matter sounded well.

"And what is the business?" she asked, in a tone of voice intended to be indifferent, but which nevertheless showed that she listened anxiously for an answer to her question.

They were both standing with their arms upon the wall, looking down upon the town of Le Puy; but they had so stood that each could see the other's countenance as they talked. Mrs. Thompson could now perceive that M. Lacordaire became red in the face, as he paused before answering her. She was near to him, and seeing his emotion gently touched his arm with her hand. This she did to reassure him, for she saw that he was ashamed of having to declare that he was a trades- man. As for herself, she had made up her mind to bear with this, if she found, as she felt sure she would find, that the trade was one which would not degrade either him or her. Hitherto, indeed,—in her early days,—she had looked down on trade; but of what benefit had her grand ideas been to her when she had returned to Eng- land? She had tried her hand at English genteel society, and no one had seemed to care for her. Therefore, she touched his arm lightly with her fingers that she might encourage him.

He paused for a moment, as I have said, and became red; and then feeling that he had shown some symp- toms of shame—and feeling also, probably, that it was unmanly in him to do so, he shook himself slightly, raised his head up somewhat more proudly than was his wont, looked her full in the face with more strength of character than she had yet seen him assume; and then, declared his business.

"Madame," he said, in a very audible, but not in a loud voice, "madame—je suis tailleur." And having so spo- ken, he turned slightly from her and looked down over the valley towards Le Puy.

There was nothing more said upon the subject as they drove down from the rock of Polignac back to the town. Immediately on receiving the announcement, Mrs. Thompson found that she had no answer to make. She withdrew her hand—and felt at once that she had re- ceived a blow. It was not that she was angry with M. Lacordaire for being a tailor; nor was she angry with him in that, being a tailor, he had so addressed her. But she was surprised, disappointed, and altogether put beyond her ease. She had, at any rate, not expected this. She had dreamed of his being a banker; thought that, perhaps, he might have been a wine merchant; but her idea had never gone below a jeweller or watchmaker. When those words broke upon her ear, "Madame, je suis tailleur," she had felt herself to be speechless.

But the words had not been a minute spoken when Lilian and Mimmy ran up to their mother. "Oh, mamma," said Lilian, "we thought you were lost; we have searched for you all over the chateau."

"We have been sitting very quietly here, my dear, looking at the view," said Mrs. Thompson.

"But, mamma, I do wish you'd see the mouth of the oracle. It is so large, and so round, and so ugly. I put my arm into it all the way," said Mimmy.

But at the present moment her mamma felt no interest in the mouth of the oracle; and so they all walked down together to the carriage. And, though the way was steep, Mrs. Thompson managed to pick her steps without the assistance of an arm; nor did M. Lacordaire presume to offer it.

The drive back to town was very silent. Mrs. Thompson did make one or two attempts at conversation, but they were not effectual. M. Lacordaire could not speak at his ease till this matter was settled, and he already had begun to perceive that his business was against him. Why is it that the trade of a tailor should be less honourable than that of a haberdasher, or even a grocer?

They sat next each other at dinner, as usual; and here, as all eyes were upon them, they both made a great struggle to behave in their accustomed way. But even in this they failed. All the world of the Hotel des Ambassadeurs knew that M. Lacordaire had gone forth to make an offer to Mrs. Thompson, and all that world, therefore, was full of speculation. But all the world could make nothing of it. M. Lacordaire did look like a rejected man, but Mrs. Thompson did not look like the woman who had rejected him. That the offer had been made—in that everybody agreed, from the senior habitue of the house who always sat at the head of the table, down to the junior assistant garcon. But as to reading the riddle, there was no accord among them.

When the dessert was done, Mrs. Thompson, as usual, withdrew, and M. Lacordaire, as usual, bowed as he stood behind his own chair. He did not, however, attempt to follow her.

But when she reached the door she called him. He was at her side in a moment, and then she whispered in his ear -

"And I, also—I will be of the same business."

When M. Lacordaire regained the table the senior habitue, the junior garcon, and all the intermediate ranks of men at the Hotel des Ambassadeurs knew that they might congratulate him.

Mrs. Thompson had made a great struggle; but, speaking for myself, I am inclined to think that she arrived at last at a wise decision.

The Courtship of
Susan Bell

The Courtship of
Susan Bell

*J*OHN MUNROE BELL had been a lawyer in Albany, State of New York, and as such had thriven well. He had thriven well as long as thrift and thriving on this earth had been allowed to him. But the Almighty had seen fit to shorten his span.

Early in life he had married a timid, anxious, pretty, good little wife, whose whole heart and mind had been given up to do his bidding and deserve his love. She had not only deserved it but had possessed it, and as long as John Munroe Bell had lived, Henrietta Bell—Hetta as he called her—had been a woman rich in blessings. After twelve years of such blessings he had left her, and had left with her two daughters, a second Hetta, and the heroine of our little story, Susan Bell.

A lawyer in Albany may thrive passing well for eight or ten years, and yet not leave behind him any very large sum of money if he dies at the end of that time. Some small modicum, some few thousand dollars, John Bell had amassed, so that his widow and daughters were not absolutely driven to look for work or bread.

In those happy days when cash had begun to flow in plenteously to the young father of the family, he had taken it into his head to build for himself, or rather for his young female brood, a small neat house in the outskirts of Saratoga Springs. In doing so he was instigated as much by the excellence of the investment for his pocket as by the salubrity of the place for his girls. He furnished the house well, and then during some summer weeks his wife lived there, and sometimes he let it.

How the widow grieved when the lord of her heart and master of her mind was laid in the grave, I need not tell. She had already counted ten years of widowhood, and her children had grown to be young women beside her at the time of which I am now about to speak. Since that sad day on which they had left Albany they had lived together at the cottage at the Springs. In winter their life had been lonely enough; but as soon as the hot weather began to drive the fainting citizens out from New York, they had always received two or three boarders—old ladies generally, and occasionally an old gentleman—persons of very steady habits, with whose pockets the widow's moderate demands agreed better than the hotel charges. And so the Bells lived for ten years.

That Saratoga is a gay place in July, August, and September, the world knows well enough. To girls who go there with trunks full of muslin and crinoline, for whom a carriage and pair of horses is always waiting immediately after dinner, whose fathers' pockets are bursting with dollars, it is a very gay place. Dancing and flirtations come as a matter of course, and matrimony follows after with only too great rapidity. But the place was not very gay for Hetta or Susan Bell.

In the first place the widow was a timid woman, and among other fears feared greatly that she should be thought guilty of setting traps for husbands. Poor mothers! how often are they charged with this sin when their honest desires go no further than that their bairns may be "respectit like the lave." And then she feared flirtations; flirtations that should be that and nothing more, flirtations that are so destructive of the heart's sweetest essence. She feared love also, though she longed for that as well as feared it;—for her girls, I mean; all such feelings for herself were long laid under ground;—and then, like a timid creature as she was, she had other indefinite fears, and among them a great fear that those girls of hers would be left husbandless,—a phase of life which after her twelve years of bliss she regarded as anything but desirable. But the upshot was,—the upshot of so many fears and such small means,—that Hetta and Susan Bell had but a dull life of it.

Were it not that I am somewhat closely restricted in the number of my pages, I would describe at full the merits and beauties of Hetta and Susan Bell. As it is I can but say a few words. At our period of their lives Hetta was nearly one-and-twenty, and Susan was just nineteen. Hetta was a short, plump, demure young woman, with the softest smoothed hair, and the brownest brightest eyes. She was very useful in the house, good at corn cakes, and thought much, particularly in these latter months, of her religious duties. Her sister in the privacy of their own little room would sometimes twit her with the admiring patience with which she would listen to the lengthened eloquence of Mr. Phineas Beckard, the Baptist minister. Now Mr. Phineas Beckard was a bachelor.

Susan was not so good a girl in the kitchen or about the house as was her sister; but she was bright in the parlour, and if that motherly heart could have been made to give out its inmost secret—which however, it could not have been made to give out in any way painful to dear Hetta—perhaps it might have been found that Susan was loved with the closest love. She was taller than her sister, and lighter; her eyes were blue as were her mother's; her hair was brighter than Hetta's, but not always so singularly neat. She had a dimple on her chin, whereas Hetta had none; dimples on her cheeks too, when she smiled; and, oh, such a mouth! There; my allowance of pages permits no more.

One piercing cold winter's day there came knocking at the widow's door—a young man. Winter days, when the ice of January is refrozen by the wind of February, are very cold at Saratoga Springs. In these days there was not often much to disturb the serenity of Mrs. Bell's house; but on the day in question there came knocking at the door—a young man.

Mrs. Bell kept an old domestic, who had lived with them in those happy Albany days. Her name was Kate O'Brien, but though picturesque in name she was hardly so in person. She was a thick-set, noisy, good-natured old Irishwoman, who had joined her lot to that of Mrs. Bell when the latter first began housekeeping, and knowing when she was well off; had remained in the same place from that day forth. She had known Hetta as a baby, and, so to say, had seen Susan's birth.

"And what might you be wanting, sir?" said Kate O'Brien, apparently not quite pleased as she opened the door and let in all the cold air.

"I wish to see Mrs. Bell. Is not this Mrs. Bell's house?" said the young man, shaking the snow from out of the breast of his coat.

He did see Mrs. Bell, and we will now tell who he was, and why he had come, and how it came to pass that his carpet-bag was brought down to the widow's house and one of the front bedrooms was prepared for him, and that he drank tea that night in the widow's parlour.

His name was Aaron Dunn, and by profession he was an engineer. What peculiar misfortune in those days of frost and snow had befallen the line of rails which runs from Schenectady to Lake Champlain, I never quite understood. Banks and bridges had in some way come to grief, and on Aaron Dunn's shoulders was thrown the burden of seeing that they were duly repaired. Saratoga Springs was the centre of these mishaps, and therefore at Saratoga Springs it was necessary that he should take up his temporary abode.

Now there was at that time in New York city a Mr. Bell, great in railway matters—an uncle of the once thriving but now departed Albany lawyer. He was a rich man, but he liked his riches himself; or at any rate had not found himself called upon to share them with the widow and daughters of his nephew. But when it chanced to come to pass that he had a hand in despatching Aaron Dunn to Saratoga, he took the young man aside and recommended him to lodge with the widow. "There," said he, "show her my card." So much the rich uncle thought he might vouchsafe to do for the nephew's widow.

Mrs. Bell and both her daughters were in the parlour when Aaron Dunn was shown in, snow and all. He told his story in a rough, shaky voice, for his teeth chattered; and he gave the card, almost wishing that he had gone to the empty big hotel, for the widow's welcome was not at first quite warm.

The widow listened to him as he gave his message, and then she took the card and looked at it. Hetta, who was sitting on the side of the fireplace facing the door, went on demurely with her work. Susan gave one glance round—her back was to the stranger—and then another; and then she moved her chair a little nearer to the wall, so as to give the young man room to come to the fire, if he would. He did not come, but his eyes glanced upon Susan Bell; and he thought that the old man in New York was right, and that the big hotel would be cold and dull. It was a pretty face to look on that cold evening as she turned it up from the stocking she was mending.

"Perhaps you don't wish to take winter boarders, ma'am?" said Aaron Dunn.

"We never have done so yet, sir," said Mrs. Bell timidly. Could she let this young wolf in among her lamb-fold? He might be a wolf;—who could tell?

"Mr. Bell seemed to think it would suit," said Aaron.

Had he acquiesced in her timidity and not pressed the point, it would have been all up with him. But the widow did not like to go against the big uncle; and so she said, "Perhaps it may, sir."

"I guess it will, finely," said Aaron. And then the widow seeing that the matter was so far settled, put down her work and came round into the passage. Hetta followed her, for there would be housework to do. Aaron gave himself another shake, settled the weekly number of dollars—with very little difficulty on his part, for he had caught another glance at Susan's face; and then went after his bag. 'Twas thus that Aaron Dunn obtained an entrance into Mrs. Bell's house. "But what if he be a wolf?" she said to herself over and over again that night, though not exactly in those words. Ay, but there is another side to that question. What if he be a stalwart man, honest-minded, with clever eye, cunning hand, ready brain, broad back, and warm heart; in want of a wife mayhap; a man that can earn his own bread and another's;—half a dozen others' when the half dozen come? Would not that be a good sort of lodger? Such a question as that too did flit, just flit, across the widow's sleepless mind. But then she thought so much more of the wolf! Wolves, she had taught herself to think, were more common than stalwart, honest-minded, wife-desirous men.

"I wonder mother consented to take him," said Hetta, when they were in the little room together.

"And why shouldn't she?" said Susan. "It will be a help."

"Yes, it will be a little help," said Hetta. "But we have done very well hitherto without winter lodgers."

"But uncle Bell said she was to."

"What is uncle Bell to us?" said Hetta, who had a spirit of her own. And she began to surmise within herself whether Aaron Dunn would join the Baptist congregation, and whether Phineas Beckard would approve of this new move.

"He is a very well-behaved young man at any rate," said Susan, "and he draws beautifully. Did you see those things he was doing?"

"He draws very well, I dare say," said Hetta, who regarded this as but a poor warranty for good behaviour. Hetta also had some fear of wolves—not for herself perhaps; but for her sister.

Aaron Dunn's work—the commencement of his work—lay at some distance from the Springs, and he left every morning with a lot of workmen by an early train—almost before daylight. And every morning, cold and wintry as the mornings were, the widow got him his breakfast with her own hands. She took his dollars and would not leave him altogether to the awkward mercies of Kate O'Brien; nor would she trust her girls to attend upon the young man. Hetta she might have trusted; but then Susan would have asked why she was spared her share of such hardship.

In the evening, leaving his work when it was dark, Aaron always returned, and then the evening was passed together. But they were passed with the most demure propriety. These women would make the tea, cut the bread and butter, and then sew; while Aaron Dunn, when the cups were removed, would always go to his plans and drawings.

On Sundays they were more together; but even on this day there was cause of separation, for Aaron went to the Episcopalian church, rather to the disgust of Hetta. In the afternoon, however, they were together; and then Phineas Beckard came in to tea on Sundays, and he and Aaron got to talking on religion; and though they disagreed pretty much, and would not give an inch either one or the other, nevertheless the minister told the widow, and Hetta too probably, that the lad had good stuff in him, though he was so stiff-necked.

"But he should be more modest in talking on such matters with a minister," said Hetta.

The Rev. Phineas acknowledged that perhaps he should; but he was honest enough to repeat that the lad had stuff in him. "Perhaps after all he is not a wolf," said the widow to herself.

Things went on in this way for above a month. Aaron had declared to himself over and over again that that face was sweet to look upon, and had unconsciously promised to himself certain delights in talking and perhaps walking with the owner of it. But the walkings had not been achieved—nor even the talkings as yet. The truth was that Dunn was bashful with young women, though he could be so stiff-necked with the minister.

And then he felt angry with himself, inasmuch as he had advanced no further; and as he lay in his bed—which perhaps those pretty hands had helped to make—he resolved that he would be a thought bolder in his bearing. He had no idea of making love to Susan Bell; of course not. But why should he not amuse himself by talking to a pretty girl when she sat so near him, evening after evening?

"What a very quiet young man he is," said Susan to her sister.

"He has his bread to earn, and sticks to his work," said Hetta. "No doubt he has his amusement when he is in the city," added the elder sister, not wishing to leave too strong an impression of the young man's virtue.

They had all now their settled places in the parlour. Hetta sat on one side of the fire, close to the table, having that side to herself. There she sat always busy. She must have made every dress and bit of linen worn in the house, and hemmed every sheet and towel, so busy was she always. Sometimes, once in a week or so, Phineas Beckard would come in, and then place was made for him between Hetta's usual seat and the table. For when there he would read out loud. On the other side, close also to the table, sat the widow, busy, but not savagely busy as her elder daughter. Between Mrs. Bell and the wall, with her feet ever on the fender, Susan used to sit; not absolutely idle, but doing work of some slender pretty sort, and talking ever and anon to her mother. Opposite to them all, at the other side of the table, far away from the fire, would Aaron Dunn place himself with his plans and drawings before him.

"Are you a judge of bridges, ma'am?" said Aaron, the evening after he had made his resolution. 'Twas thus he began his courtship.

"Of bridges?" said Mrs. Bell—"oh dear no, sir." But she put out her hand to take the little drawing which Aaron handed to her.

"Because that's one I've planned for our bit of a new branch from Moreau up to Lake George. I guess Miss Susan knows something about bridges."

"I guess I don't," said Susan—"only that they oughtn't to tumble down when the frost comes."

"Ha, ha, ha; no more they ought. I'll tell McEvoy that." McEvoy had been a former engineer on the line. "Well, that won't burst with any frost, I guess."

"Oh my! how pretty!" said the widow, and then Susan of course jumped up to look over her mother's shoulder.

The artful dodger! he had drawn and coloured a beautiful little sketch of a bridge; not an engineer's plan with sections and measurements, vexatious to a woman's eye, but a graceful little bridge with a string of cars running under it. You could almost hear the bell going.

"Well; that is a pretty bridge," said Susan. "Isn't it, Hetta?"

"I don't know anything about bridges," said Hetta, to whose clever eyes the dodge was quite apparent. But in spite of her cleverness Mrs. Bell and Susan had soon moved their chairs round to the table, and were looking through the contents of Aaron's portfolio. "But yet he may be a wolf," thought the poor widow, just as she was kneeling down to say her prayers.

That evening certainly made a commencement. Though Hetta went on pertinaciously with the body of a new dress, the other two ladies did not put in another stitch that night. From his drawings Aaron got to his instruments, and before bedtime was teaching Susan how to draw parallel lines. Susan found that she had quite an aptitude for parallel lines, and altogether had a good time of it that evening. It is dull to go on week after week, and month after month, talking only to one's mother and sister. It is dull though one does not oneself recognise it to be so. A little change in such matters is so very pleasant. Susan had not the slightest idea of regarding Aaron as even a possible lover. But young ladies do like the conversation of young gentlemen. Oh, my exceedingly proper prim old lady, you who are so shocked at this as a general doctrine, has it never occurred to you that the Creator has so intended it?

Susan understanding little of the how and why, knew that she had had a good time, and was rather in spirits as she went to bed. But Hetta had been frightened by the dodge.

"Oh, Hetta, you should have looked at those drawings. He is so clever!" said Susan.

"I don't know that they would have done me much good," replied Hetta.

"Good! Well, they'd do me more good than a long sermon, I know," said Susan; "except on a Sunday, of course," she added apologetically. This was an ill-tempered attack both on Hetta and Hetta's admirer. But then why had Hetta been so snappish?

"I'm sure he's a wolf;" thought Hetta as she went to bed.

"What a very clever young man he is!" thought Susan to herself as she pulled the warm clothes round about her shoulders and ears.

"Well that certainly was an improvement," thought Aaron as he went through the same operation, with a stronger feeling of self-approbation than he had enjoyed for some time past.

In the course of the next fortnight the family arrangements all altered themselves. Unless when Beckard was there Aaron would sit in the widow's place, the widow would take Susan's chair, and the two girls would be opposite. And then Dunn would read to them; not sermons, but passages from Shakspeare, and Byron, and Longfellow. "He reads much better than Mr. Beckard," Susan had said one night. "Of course you're a competent judge!" had been Hetta's retort. "I mean that I like it better," said Susan. "It's well that all people don't think alike," replied Hetta.

And then there was a deal of talking. The widow herself, as unconscious in this respect as her youngest daughter, certainly did find that a little variety was agreeable on those long winter nights; and talked herself with unaccustomed freedom. And Beckard came there oftener and talked very much. When he was there the two young men did all the talking, and they pounded each other immensely. But still there grew up a sort of friendship between them.

"Mr. Beckard seems quite to take to him," said Mrs. Bell to her eldest daughter.

"It is his great good nature, mother," replied Hetta.

It was at the end of the second month when Aaron took another step in advance—a perilous step. Sometimes on evenings he still went on with his drawing for an hour or so; but during three or four evenings he never asked any one to look at what he was doing. On one Friday he sat over his work till late, without any reading or talking at all; so late that at last Mrs. Bell said, "If you're going to sit much longer, Mr. Dunn, I'll get you to put out the candles." Thereby showing, had he known it or had she, that the mother's confidence in the young man was growing fast. Hetta knew all about it, and dreaded that the growth was too quick.

"I've finished now," said Aaron; and he looked carefully at the cardboard on which he had been washing in his water-colours. "I've finished now." He then hesitated a moment; but ultimately he put the card into his portfolio and carried it up to his bedroom. Who does not perceive that it was intended as a present to Susan Bell?

The question which Aaron asked himself that night, and which he hardly knew how to answer, was this. Should he offer the drawing to Susan in the presence of her mother and sister, or on some occasion when they two might be alone together? No such occasion had ever yet occurred, but Aaron thought that it might probably be brought about. But then he wanted to make no fuss about it. His first intention had been to chuck the drawing lightly across the table when it was completed, and so make nothing of it. But he had finished it with more care than he had at first intended; and then he had hesitated when he had finished it. It was too late now for that plan of chucking it over the table.

On the Saturday evening when he came down from his room, Mr. Beckard was there, and there was no opportunity that night. On the Sunday, in conformity with a previous engagement, he went to hear Mr. Beckard preach, and walked to and from meeting with the family. This pleased Mrs. Bell, and they were all very gracious that afternoon. But Sunday was no day for the picture.

On Monday the thing had become of importance to him. Things always do when they are kept over. Before

tea that evening when he came down Mrs. Bell and Susan only were in the room. He knew Hetta for his foe,
and therefore determined to use this occasion.

"Miss Susan," he said, stammering somewhat, and
blushing too, poor fool! "I have done a little drawing
which I want you to accept," and he put his portfolio
down on the table.

"Oh! I don't know," said Susan, who had seen the blush.

Mrs. Bell had seen the blush also, and pursed her mouth
up, and looked grave. Had there been no stammering
and no blush, she might have thought nothing of it.

Aaron saw at once that his little gift was not to go down
smoothly. He was, however, in for it now, so he picked it
out from among the other papers in the case and brought
it over to Susan. He endeavoured to hand it to her with an
air of indifference, but I cannot say that he succeeded.

It was a very pretty, well-finished, water-coloured
drawing, representing still the same bridge, but with
more adjuncts. In Susan's eyes it was a work of high
art. Of pictures probably she had seen but little, and
her liking for the artist no doubt added to her admira-
tion. But the more she admired it and wished for it, the
stronger was her feeling that she ought not to take it.

Poor Susan! she stood for a minute looking at the drawing, but she said nothing; not even a word of praise.
She felt that she was red in the face, and uncourteous
to their lodger; but her mother was looking at her and
she did not know how to behave herself.

Mrs. Bell put out her hand for the sketch, trying to be-
think herself as she did so in what least uncivil way she
could refuse the present. She took a moment to look at

it collecting her thoughts, and as she did so her woman's wit came to her aid.

"Oh dear, Mr. Dunn, it is very pretty; quite a beautiful picture. I cannot let Susan rob you of that. You must keep that for some of your own particular friends."

"But I did it for her," said Aaron innocently.

Susan looked down at the ground, half pleased at the declaration. The drawing would look very pretty in a small gilt frame put over her dressing-table. But the matter now was altogether in her mother's hands.

"I am afraid it is too valuable, sir, for Susan to accept."

"It is not valuable at all," said Aaron, declining to take it back from the widow's hand.

"Oh, I am quite sure it is. It is worth ten dollars at least—or twenty," said poor Mrs. Bell, not in the very best taste. But she was perplexed, and did not know how to get out of the scrape. The article in question now lay upon the table-cloth, appropriated by no one, and at this moment Hetta came into the room.

"It is not worth ten cents," said Aaron, with something like a frown on his brow. "But as we had been talking about the bridge, I thought Miss Susan would accept it."

"Accept what?" said Hetta. And then her eye fell upon the drawing and she took it up.

"It is beautifully done," said Mrs. Bell, wishing much to soften the matter; perhaps the more so that Hetta the demure was now present. "I am telling Mr. Dunn that we can't take a present of anything so valuable."

"Oh dear no," said Hetta. "It wouldn't be right."

It was a cold frosty evening in March, and the fire was burning brightly on the hearth. Aaron Dunn took up the drawing quietly—very quietly—and rolling it up, as such drawings are rolled, put it between the blazing logs. It was the work of four evenings, and his chef-d'oeuvre in the way of art.

Susan, when she saw what he had done, burst out into tears. The widow could very readily have done so also, but she was able to refrain herself, and merely exclaimed—"Oh, Mr. Dunn!"

"If Mr. Dunn chooses to burn his own picture, he has certainly a right to do so," said Hetta.

Aaron immediately felt ashamed of what he had done; and he also could have cried, but for his manliness. He walked away to one of the parlour-windows, and looked out upon the frosty night. It was dark, but the stars were bright, and he thought that he should like to be walking fast by himself along the line of rails towards Balston. There he stood, perhaps for three minutes. He thought it would be proper to give Susan time to recover from her tears.

"Will you please to come to your tea, sir?" said the soft voice of Mrs. Bell.

He turned round to do so, and found that Susan was gone. It was not quite in her power to recover from her tears in three minutes. And then the drawing had been so beautiful! It had been done expressly for her too! And there had been something, she knew not what, in his eye as he had so declared. She had watched him intently over those four evenings' work, wondering why he did not show it, till her feminine curiosity had become rather strong. It was something very particular, she was sure, and she had learned that all that precious work had been for her. Now all that precious work was destroyed. How was it possible that she should not cry for more than three minutes?

The others took their meal in perfect silence, and when it was over the two women sat down to their work. Aaron had a book which he pretended to read, but instead of reading he was bethinking himself that he had behaved badly. What right had he to throw them all into such confusion by indulging in his passion? He was ashamed of what he had done, and fancied that Susan would hate him. Fancying that, he began to find at the same time that he by no means hated her.

At last Hetta got up and left the room. She knew that her sister was sitting alone in the cold, and Hetta was affectionate. Susan had not been in fault, and therefore Hetta went up to console her.

"Mrs. Bell," said Aaron, as soon as the door was closed, "I beg your pardon for what I did just now."

"Oh, sir, I'm so sorry that the picture is burnt," said poor Mrs. Bell.

"The picture does not matter a straw," said Aaron. "But I see that I have disturbed you all,—and I am afraid I have made Miss Susan unhappy."

"She was grieved because your picture was burnt," said Mrs. Bell, putting some emphasis on the "your," intending to show that her daughter had not regarded the drawing as her own. But the emphasis bore another meaning; and so the widow perceived as soon as she had spoken.

"Oh, I can do twenty more of the same if anybody wanted them," said Aaron. "If I do another like it, will you let her take it, Mrs. Bell?—just to show that you have forgiven me, and that we are friends as we were before?"

Was he, or was he not a wolf? That was the question which Mrs. Bell scarcely knew how to answer. Hetta had given her voice, saying he was lupine. Mr. Beckard's opinion she had not liked to ask directly. Mr. Beckard she thought would probably propose to Hetta; but as yet he had not done so. And, as he was still a stranger in the family, she did not like in any way to compromise Susan's name. Indirectly she had asked the question, and, indirectly also, Mr. Beckard's answer had been favourable.

"But it mustn't mean anything, sir," was the widow's weak answer, when she had paused on the question for a moment.

"Oh no, of course not," said Aaron, joyously, and his face became radiant and happy. "And I do beg your pardon for burning it; and the young ladies' pardon too." And then he rapidly got out his cardboard, and set himself to work about another bridge. The widow, meditating many things in her heart, commenced the hemming of a handkerchief.

In about an hour the two girls came back to the room and silently took their accustomed places. Aaron hardly looked up, but went on diligently with his drawing. This bridge should be a better bridge than that other. Its acceptance was now assured. Of course it was to mean nothing. That was a matter of course. So he worked away diligently, and said nothing to anybody.

When they went off to bed the two girls went into the mother's room. "Oh, mother, I hope he is not very angry," said Susan.

"Angry!" said Hetta, "if anybody should be angry, it is mother. He ought to have known that Susan could not accept it. He should never have offered it."

"But he's doing another," said Mrs. Bell.

"Not for her," said Hetta.

"Yes he is," said Mrs. Bell, "and I have promised that she shall take it." Susan as she heard this sank gently into the chair behind her, and her eyes became full of tears. The intimation was almost too much for her.

"Oh, mother!" said Hetta.

"But I particularly said that it was to mean nothing."

"Oh, mother, that makes it worse."

Why should Hetta interfere in this way, thought Susan to herself. Had she interfered when Mr. Beckard gave Hetta a testament bound in Morocco? had not she smiled, and looked gratified, and kissed her sister, and declared that Phineas Beckard was a nice dear man, and by far the most elegant preacher at the Springs? Why should Hetta be so cruel?

"I don't see that, my dear," said the mother. Hetta would not explain before her sister, so they all went to bed.

On the Thursday evening the drawing was finished. Not a word had been said about it, at any rate in his presence, and he had gone on working in silence. "There," said he, late on the Thursday evening, "I don't know that it will be any better if I go on daubing for another hour. There, Miss Susan; there's another bridge. I hope that will neither burst with the frost, nor yet be destroyed by fire," and he gave it a light flip with his fingers and sent it skimming over the table.

Susan blushed and smiled, and took it up. "Oh, it is beautiful," she said. "Isn't it beautifully done, mother?" and then all the three got up to look at it, and all confessed that it was excellently done.

"And I am sure we are very much obliged to you," said Susan after a pause, remembering that she had not yet thanked him.

"Oh, it's nothing," said he, not quite liking the word "we." On the following day he returned from his work to Saratoga about noon. This he had never done before, and therefore no one expected that he would be seen in the house before the evening. On this occasion, however, he went straight thither, and as chance would have it, both the widow and her elder daughter were out. Susan was there alone in charge of the house.

He walked in and opened the parlour door. There she sat, with her feet on the fender, with her work unheeded on the table behind her, and the picture, Aaron's drawing, lying on her knees. She was gazing at it intently as he entered, thinking in her young heart that it possessed all the beauties which a picture could possess.

"Oh, Mr. Dunn," she said, getting up and holding the telltale sketch behind the skirt of her dress.

"Miss Susan, I have come here to tell your mother that I must start for New York this afternoon and be there for six weeks, or perhaps longer."

"Mother is out," said she; "I'm so sorry."

"Is she?" said Aaron.

"And Hetta too. Dear me. And you'll be wanting dinner. I'll go and see about it."

Aaron began to swear that he could not possibly eat any dinner. He had dined once, and was going to dine again;—anything to keep her from going.

"But you must have something, Mr. Dunn," and she walked towards the door.

But he put his back to it. "Miss Susan," said he, "I guess I've been here nearly two months."

"Yes, sir, I believe you have," she replied, shaking in her shoes, and not knowing which way to look.

"And I hope we have been good friends."

"Yes, sir," said Susan, almost beside herself as to what she was saying.

"I'm going away now, and it seems to be such a time before I'll be back."

"Will it, Sir?"

"Six weeks, Miss Susan!" and then he paused, looking into her eyes, to see what he could read there. She leant against the table, pulling to pieces a morsel of half-ravelled muslin which she held in her hand; but her eyes were turned to the ground, and he could hardly see them.

"Miss Susan," he continued, "I may as well speak out now as at another time." He too was looking towards the ground, and clearly did not know what to do with his hands. "The truth is just this. I—I love you dearly, with all my heart. I never saw any one I ever thought so beautiful, so nice, and so good;—and what's more, I never shall. I'm not very good at this sort of thing, I know; but I couldn't go away from Saratoga for six weeks and not tell you." And then he ceased. He did not ask for any love in return. His presumption had not got so far as that yet. He merely declared his passion, leaning against the door, and there he stood twiddling his thumbs.

Susan had not the slightest conception of the way in which she ought to receive such a declaration. She had never had a lover before; nor had she ever thought of Aaron absolutely as a lover, though something very like love for him had been crossing over her spirit. Now, at this moment, she felt that he was the beau-ideal of manhood, though his boots were covered with the railway mud, and though his pantaloons were tucked up in rolls round his ankles. He was a fine, well-grown, open-faced fellow, whose eye was bold and yet tender, whose brow was full and broad, and all his bearing manly. Love him! Of course she loved him. Why else had her heart melted with pleasure when her mother said that that second picture was to be accepted?

But what was she to say? Anything but the open truth; she well knew that. The open truth would not do at all. What would her mother say and Hetta if she were rashly to say that? Hetta, she knew, would be dead against such a lover, and of her mother's approbation she had hardly more hope. Why they should disapprove of Aaron as a lover she had never asked herself. There are many nice things that seem to be wrong only because they are so nice. Maybe that Susan regarded a lover as one of them. "Oh, Mr. Dunn, you shouldn't." That in fact was all that she could say.

"Should not I?" said he. "Well, perhaps not; but there's the truth, and no harm ever comes of that. Perhaps I'd better not ask you for an answer now, but I thought it better you should know it all. And remember this—I only care for one thing now in the world, and that is for your love." And then he paused, thinking possibly that in spite of what he had said he might perhaps get some sort of an answer, some inkling of the state of her heart's disposition towards him.

But Susan had at once resolved to take him at his word when he suggested that an immediate reply was not necessary. To say that she loved him was of course impossible, and to say that she did not was equally so.

She determined therefore to close at once with the offer of silence.

When he ceased speaking there was a moment's pause, during which he strove hard to read what might be written on her down-turned face. But he was not good at such reading. "Well, I guess I'll go and get my things ready now," he said, and then turned round to open the door.

"Mother will be in before you are gone, I suppose," said Susan.

"I have only got twenty minutes," said he, looking at his watch. "But, Susan, tell her what I have said to you. Goodbye." And he put out his hand. He knew he should see her again, but this had been his plan to get her hand in his.

"Good-bye, Mr. Dunn," and she gave him her hand.

He held it tight for a moment, so that she could not draw it away,—could not if she would. "Will you tell your mother?" he asked.

"Yes," she answered, quite in a whisper. "I guess I'd better tell her." And then she gave a long sigh. He pressed her hand again and got it up to his lips.

"Mr. Dunn, don't," she said. But he did kiss it. "God bless you, my own dearest, dearest girl! I'll just open the door as I come down. Perhaps Mrs. Bell will be here." And then he rushed up stairs.

But Mrs. Bell did not come in. She and Hetta were at a weekly service at Mr. Beckard's meeting-house, and Mr. Beckard it seemed had much to say. Susan, when left alone, sat down and tried to think. But she could not think; she could only love. She could use her mind only in recounting to herself the perfections of that demigod whose heavy steps were so audible overhead, as he walked to and fro collecting his things and putting them into his bag.

And then, just when he had finished, she bethought herself that he must be hungry. She flew to the kitchen, but she was too late. Before she could even reach at the loaf of bread he descended the stairs, with a clattering noise, and heard her voice as she spoke quickly to Kate O'Brien.

"Miss Susan," he said, "don't get anything for me, for I'm off."

"Oh, Mr. Dunn, I am so sorry. You'll be so hungry on your journey," and she came out to him in the passage.

"I shall want nothing on the journey, dearest, if you'll say one kind word to me."

Again her eyes went to the ground. "What do you want me to say, Mr. Dunn?"

"Say, God bless you, Aaron."

"God bless you, Aaron," said she; and yet she was sure that she had not declared her love. He however thought otherwise, and went up to New York with a happy heart.

Things happened in the next fortnight rather quickly. Susan at once resolved to tell her mother, but she resolved also not to tell Hetta. That afternoon she got her mother to herself in Mrs. Bell's own room, and then she made a clean breast of it.

"And what did you say to him, Susan?"

"I said nothing, mother."

"Nothing, dear!"

"No, mother; not a word. He told me he didn't want it."
She forgot how she had used his Christian name in bidding God bless him.

"Oh dear!" said the widow.

"Was it very wrong?" asked Susan.

"But what do you think yourself, my child?" asked Mrs.
Bell after a while. "What are your own feelings."

Mrs. Bell was sitting on a chair and Susan was standing opposite to her against the post of the bed. She made no answer, but moving from her place, she threw herself into her mother's arms, and hid her face on her mother's shoulder. It was easy enough to guess what were her feelings.

"But, my darling," said her mother, "you must not think that it is an engagement."

"No," said Susan, sorrowfully.

"Young men say those things to amuse themselves."
Wolves, she would have said, had she spoken out her mind freely.

"Oh, mother, he is not like that."

The daughter contrived to extract a promise from the mother that Hetta should not be told just at present.
Mrs. Bell calculated that she had six weeks before her; as yet Mr. Beckard had not spoken out, but there was reason to suppose that he would do so before those six weeks would be over, and then she would be able to seek counsel from him.

Mr. Beckard spoke out at the end of six days, and Hetta frankly accepted him. "I hope you'll love your brother-in-law," said she to Susan.

"Oh, I will indeed," said Susan; and in the softness of her heart at the moment she almost made up her mind to tell; but Hetta was full of her own affairs, and thus it passed off.

It was then arranged that Hetta should go and spend a week with Mr. Beckard's parents. Old Mr. Beckard was a farmer living near Utica, and now that the match was declared and approved, it was thought well that Hetta should know her future husband's family. So she went for a week, and Mr. Beckard went with her. "He will be back in plenty of time for me to speak to him before Aaron Dunn's six weeks are over," said Mrs. Bell to herself.

But things did not go exactly as she expected. On the very morning after the departure of the engaged couple, there came a letter from Aaron, saying that he would be at Saratoga that very evening. The railway people had ordered him down again for some days' special work; then he was to go elsewhere, and not to return to Saratoga till June. "But he hoped," so said the letter, "that Mrs. Bell would not turn him into the street even then, though the summer might have come, and her regular lodgers might be expected."

"Oh dear, oh dear!" said Mrs. Bell to herself, reflecting that she had no one of whom she could ask advice, and that she must decide that very day. Why had she let Mr. Beckard go without telling him? Then she told Susan, and Susan spent the day trembling. Perhaps, thought Mrs. Bell, he will say nothing about it. In such case, however, would it not be her duty to say something? Poor mother! She trembled nearly as much as Susan.

It was dark when the fatal knock came at the door. The tea-things were already laid, and the tea-cake was already baked; for it would at any rate be necessary to give Mr. Dunn his tea. Susan, when she heard the knock, rushed from her chair and took refuge up stairs. The widow gave a long sigh and settled her dress. Kate O'Brien with willing step opened the door, and bade her old friend welcome.

"How are the ladies?" asked Aaron, trying to gather something from the face and voice of the domestic.

"Miss Hetta and Mr. Beckard be gone off to Utica, just man-and-wife like! and so they are, more power to them."

"Oh indeed; I'm very glad," said Aaron—and so he was; very glad to have Hetta the demure out of the way. And then he made his way into the parlour, doubting much, and hoping much.

Mrs. Bell rose from her chair, and tried to look grave. Aaron glancing round the room saw that Susan was not there. He walked straight up to the widow, and offered her his hand, which she took. It might be that Susan had not thought fit to tell, and in such case it would not be right for him to compromise her; so he said never a word.

But the subject was too important to the mother to allow of her being silent when the young man stood before her. "Oh, Mr. Dunn," said she, "what is this you have been saying to Susan?"

"I have asked her to be my wife," said he, drawing himself up and looking her full in the face. Mrs. Bell's heart was almost as soft as her daughter's, and it was nearly gone; but at the moment she had nothing to say but, "Oh dear, oh dear!"

"May I not call you mother?" said he, taking both her hands in his.

"Oh dear—oh dear! But will you be good to her? Oh, Aaron Dunn, if you deceive my child!"

In another quarter of an hour, Susan was kneeling at her mother's knee, with her face on her mother's lap; the mother was wiping tears out of her eyes; and Aaron was standing by holding one of the widow's hands.

"You are my mother too, now," said he. What would Hetta and Mr. Beckard say, when they came back? But then he surely was not a wolf!

There were four or five days left for courtship before Hetta and Mr. Beckard would return; four or five days during which Susan might be happy, Aaron triumphant, and Mrs. Bell nervous. Days I have said, but after all it was only the evenings that were so left. Every morning Susan got up to give Aaron his breakfast, but Mrs. Bell got up also. Susan boldly declared her right to do so, and Mrs. Bell found no objection which she could urge.

But after that Aaron was always absent till seven or eight in the evening, when he would return to his tea. Then came the hour or two of lovers' intercourse.

But they were very tame, those hours. The widow still felt an undefined fear that she was wrong, and though her heart yearned to know that her daughter was happy in the sweet happiness of accepted love, yet she dreaded to be too confident. Not a word had been said about money matters; not a word of Aaron Dunn's relatives. So she did not leave them by themselves, but waited with what patience she could for the return of her wise counsellors.

And then Susan hardly knew how to behave herself with her accepted suitor. She felt that she was very happy; but perhaps she was most happy when she was thinking about him through the long day, assisting in fixing little things for his comfort, and waiting for his evening return. And as he sat there in the parlour, she could be happy then too, if she were but allowed to sit still and look at him,—not stare at him, but raise her eyes every now and again to his face for the shortest possible glance, as she had been used to do ever since he came there.

But he, unconscionable lover, wanted to hear her speak, was desirous of being talked to, and perhaps thought that he should by rights be allowed to sit by her, and hold her hand. No such privileges were accorded to him. If they had been alone together, walking side by side on the green turf, as lovers should walk, she would soon have found the use of her tongue,—have talked fast enough no doubt. Under such circumstances, when a girl's shyness has given way to real intimacy, there is in general no end to her power of chatting. But though there was much love between Aaron and Susan, there was as yet but little intimacy. And then, let a mother be ever so motherly—and no mother could have more of a mother's tenderness than Mrs. Bell—still her presence must be a restraint. Aaron was very fond of Mrs. Bell; but nevertheless he did sometimes wish that some domestic duty would take her out of the parlour for a few happy minutes. Susan went out very often, but Mrs. Bell seemed to be a fixture.

Once for a moment he did find his love alone, immediately as he came into the house. "My own Susan, you do love me? do say so to me once." And he contrived to slip his arm round her waist. "Yes," she whispered; but she slipped like an eel from his hands, and left him only preparing himself for a kiss. And then when she got to her room, half frightened, she clasped her hands together, and bethought herself that she did really love him with a strength and depth of love which filled her whole existence. Why could she not have told him something of all this?

And so the few days of his second sojourn at Saratoga passed away, not altogether satisfactorily. It was settled that he should return to New York on Saturday night, leaving Saratoga on that evening; and as the Beckards— Hetta was already regarded quite as a Beckard—were to be back to dinner on that day, Mrs. Bell would have an opportunity of telling her wondrous tale. It might be well that Mr. Beckard should see Aaron before his departure.

On that Saturday the Beckards did arrive just in time for dinner. It may be imagined that Susan's appetite was not very keen, nor her manner very collected. But all this passed by unobserved in the importance attached to the various Beckard arrangements which came un- der discussion. Ladies and gentlemen circumstanced as were Hetta and Mr. Beckard are perhaps a little too apt to think that their own affairs are paramount. But after dinner Susan vanished at once, and when Hetta prepared to follow her, desirous of further talk about matrimonial arrangements, her mother stopped her, and the disclosure was made.

"Proposed to her!" said Hetta, who perhaps thought that one marriage in a family was enough at a time.

"Yes, my love—and he did it, I must say, in a very hon- ourable way, telling her not to make any answer till she had spoken to me;—now that was very nice; was it not, Phineas?" Mrs. Bell had become very anxious that Aaron should not be voted a wolf.

"And what has been said to him since?" asked the dis- creet Phineas.

"Why—nothing absolutely decisive." Oh, Mrs. Bell! "You see I know nothing as to his means."

"Nothing at all," said Hetta.

"He is a man that will always earn his bread," said Mr. Beckard; and Mrs. Bell blessed him in her heart for saying it.

"But has he been encouraged?" asked Hetta.

"Well; yes, he has," said the widow.

"Then Susan I suppose likes him?" asked Phineas.

"Well; yes, she does," said the widow. And the conference ended in a resolution that Phineas Beckard should have a conversation with Aaron Dunn, as to his worldly means and position; and that he, Phineas, should decide whether Aaron might, or might not be at once accepted as a lover, according to the tenor of that conversation. Poor Susan was not told anything of all this. "Better not," said Hetta the demure. "It will only flurry her the more." How would she have liked it, if without consulting her, they had left it to Aaron to decide whether or no she might marry Phineas?

They knew where on the works Aaron was to be found, and thither Mr. Beckard rode after dinner. We need not narrate at length the conference between the young men. Aaron at once declared that he had nothing but what he made as an engineer, and explained that he held no permanent situation on the line. He was well paid at that present moment, but at the end of summer he would have to look for employment.

"Then you can hardly marry quite at present," said the discreet minister.

"Perhaps not quite immediately."

"And long engagements are never wise," said the other.

"Three or four months," suggested Aaron. But Mr. Beckard shook his head.

The afternoon at Mrs. Bell's house was melancholy. The final decision of the three judges was as follows. There was to be no engagement; of course no correspondence. Aaron was to be told that it would be better that he should get lodgings elsewhere when he returned; but that he would be allowed to visit at Mrs. Bell's house,— and at Mrs. Beckard's, which was very considerate. If he should succeed in getting a permanent appointment, and if he and Susan still held the same mind, why then—&c. &c. Such was Susan's fate, as communicated to her by Mrs. Bell and Hetta. She sat still and wept when she heard it; but she did not complain. She had always felt that Hetta would be against her.

"Mayn't I see him, then?" she said through her tears.

Hetta thought she had better not. Mrs. Bell thought she might. Phineas decided that they might shake hands, but only in full conclave. There was to be no lovers' farewell. Aaron was to leave the house at half-past five; but before he went Susan should be called down. Poor Susan! She sat down and bemoaned herself; uncomplaining, but very sad.

Susan was soft, feminine, and manageable. But Aaron Dunn was not very soft, was especially masculine, and in some matters not easily manageable. When Mr. Beckard in the widow's presence—Hetta had retired in obedience to her lover—informed him of the court's decision, there came over his face the look which he had worn when he burned the picture. "Mrs. Bell," he said, "had encouraged his engagement; and he did not understand why other people should now come and disturb it."

"Not an engagement, Aaron," said Mrs. Bell piteously.

"He was able and willing to work," he said, "and knew his profession. What young man of his age had done better than he had?" and he glanced round at them with perhaps more pride than was quite becoming.

Then Mr. Beckard spoke out, very wisely no doubt, but perhaps a little too much at length. Sons and daughters, as well as fathers and mothers, will know very well what he said; so I need not repeat his words. I cannot say that Aaron listened with much attention, but he understood perfectly what the upshot of it was. Many a man understands the purport of many a sermon without listening to one word in ten. Mr. Beckard meant to be kind in his manner; indeed was so, only that Aaron could not accept as kindness any interference on his part.

"I'll tell you what, Mrs. Bell," said he. "I look upon myself as engaged to her. And I look on her as engaged to me. I tell you so fairly; and I believe that's her mind as well as mine."

"But, Aaron, you won't try to see her—or to write to her,—not in secret; will you?"

"When I try to see her, I'll come and knock at this door; and if I write to her, I'll write to her full address by the post. I never did and never will do anything in secret."

"I know you're good and honest," said the widow with her handkerchief to her eyes.

"Then why do you separate us?" asked he, almost roughly. "I suppose I may see her at any rate before I go. My time's nearly up now, I guess."

And then Susan was called for, and she and Hetta came down together. Susan crept in behind her sister. Her eyes were red with weeping, and her appearance was altogether disconsolate. She had had a lover for a week, and now she was to be robbed of him.

"Good-bye, Susan," said Aaron, and he walked up to her without bashfulness or embarrassment. Had they all been compliant and gracious to him he would have been as bashful as his love; but now his temper was hot. "Good-bye, Susan," and she took his hand, and he held hers till he had finished. "And remember this, I look upon you as my promised wife, and I don't fear that you'll deceive me. At any rate I shan't deceive you."

"Good-bye, Aaron," she sobbed.

"Good-bye, and God bless you, my own darling!" And then without saying a word to any one else, he turned his back upon them and went his way.

There had been something very consolatory, very sweet, to the poor girl in her lover's last words. And yet they had almost made her tremble. He had been so bold, and stern, and confident. He had seemed so utterly to defy the impregnable discretion of Mr. Beckard, so to despise the demure propriety of Hetta. But of this she felt sure, when she came to question her heart, that she could never, never, never cease to love him better than all the world beside. She would wait—patiently if she could find patience—and then, if he deserted her, she would die.

In another month Hetta became Mrs. Beckard. Susan brisked up a little for the occasion, and looked very pretty as bridesmaid. She was serviceable too in arranging household matters, hemming linen and sewing table-cloths; though of course in these matters she did not do a tenth of what Hetta did.

Then the summer came, the Saratoga summer of July, August, and September, during which the widow's house was full; and Susan's hands saved the pain of her heart, for she was forced into occupation. Now that Hetta was gone to her own duties, it was necessary that Susan's part in the household should be more prominent.

Aaron did not come back to his work at Saratoga. Why he did not they could not then learn. During the whole long summer they heard not a word of him nor from him; and then when the cold winter months came and their boarders had left them, Mrs. Beckard congratulated her sister in that she had given no further encouragement to a lover who cared so little for her. This was very hard to bear. But Susan did bear it.

That winter was very sad. They learned nothing of Aaron Dunn till about January; and then they heard that he was doing very well. He was engaged on the Erie trunk line, was paid highly, and was much esteemed. And yet he neither came nor sent! "He has an excellent situation," their informant told them. "And a permanent one?" asked the widow. "Oh, yes, no doubt," said the gentleman, "for I happen to know that they count greatly on him." And yet he sent no word of love.

After that the winter became very sad indeed. Mrs. Bell thought it to be her duty now to teach her daughter that in all probability she would see Aaron Dunn no more. It was open to him to leave her without being absolutely a wolf. He had been driven from the house when he was poor, and they had no right to expect that he would return, now that he had made some rise in the world. "Men do amuse themselves in that way," the widow tried to teach her.

"He is not like that, mother," she said again.

"But they do not think so much of these things as we do," urged the mother.

"Don't they?" said Susan, oh, so sorrowfully; and so through the whole long winter months she became paler and paler, and thinner and thinner.

And then Hetta tried to console her with religion, and that perhaps did not make things any better. Religious consolation is the best cure for all griefs; but it must not be looked for specially with regard to any individual sorrow. A religious man, should he become bankrupt through the misfortunes of the world, will find true consolation in his religion even for that sorrow. But a bankrupt, who has not thought much of such things, will hardly find solace by taking up religion for that special occasion.

And Hetta perhaps was hardly prudent in her attempts. She thought that it was wicked in Susan to grow thin and pale for love of Aaron Dunn, and she hardly hid her thoughts. Susan was not sure but that it might be wicked, but this doubt in no way tended to make her plump or rosy. So that in those days she found no comfort in her sister.

But her mother's pity and soft love did ease her sufferings, though it could not make them cease. Her mother did not tell her that she was wicked, or bid her read long sermons, or force her to go oftener to the meeting-house.

"He will never come again, I think," she said one day, as with a shawl wrapped around her shoulders, she leant with her head upon her mother's bosom.

"My own darling," said the mother, pressing her child closely to her side.

"You think he never will, eh, mother?" What could Mrs. Bell say? In her heart of hearts she did not think he ever would come again.

"No, my child. I do not think he will." And then the hot tears ran down, and the sobs came thick and frequent.

"My darling, my darling!" exclaimed the mother; and they wept together.

"Was I wicked to love him at the first," she asked that night.

"No, my child; you were not wicked at all. At least I think not."

"Then why—" Why was he sent away? It was on her tongue to ask that question; but she paused and spared her mother. This was as they were going to bed. The next morning Susan did not get up. She was not ill, she said; but weak and weary. Would her mother let her lie that day? And then Mrs. Bell went down alone to her room, and sorrowed with all her heart for the sorrow of her child. Why, oh why, had she driven away from her door-sill the love of an honest man?

On the next morning Susan again did not get up;—nor did she hear, or if she heard she did not recognise, the step of the postman who brought a letter to the door. Early, before the widow's breakfast, the postman came, and the letter which he brought was as follows:-

"My Dear Mrs. Bell,

"I have now got a permanent situation on the Erie line, and the salary is enough for myself and a wife. At least I think so, and I hope you will too. I shall be down at Saratoga to-morrow evening, and I hope neither Susan nor you will refuse to receive me.

"Yours affectionately,
"AARON DUNN."

That was all. It was very short, and did not contain one word of love; but it made the widow's heart leap for joy. She was rather afraid that Aaron was angry, he wrote so curtly and with such a brusque business-like attention to mere facts; but surely he could have but one object in coming there. And then he alluded specially to a wife. So the widow's heart leapt with joy.

But how was she to tell Susan? She ran up stairs almost breathless with haste, to the bedroom door; but then she stopped; too much joy she had heard was as dangerous as too much sorrow; she must think it over for a while, and so she crept back again.

But after breakfast—that is, when she had sat for a while over her teacup—she returned to the room, and this time she entered it. The letter was in her hand, but held so as to be hidden;—in her left hand as she sat down with her right arm towards the invalid.

"Susan dear," she said, and smiled at her child, "you'll be able to get up this morning? eh, dear?"

"Yes, mother," said Susan, thinking that her mother objected to this idleness of her lying in bed. And so she began to bestir herself.

"I don't mean this very moment, love. Indeed, I want to sit with you for a little while," and she put her right arm affectionately round her daughter's waist.

"Dearest mother," said Susan.

"Ah! there's one dearer than me, I guess," and Mrs. Bell smiled sweetly, as she made the maternal charge against her daughter.

Susan raised herself quickly in the bed, and looked straight into her mother's face. "Mother, mother," she said, "what is it? You've something to tell. Oh, mother!" And stretching herself over, she struck her hand against the corner of Aaron's letter. "Mother, you've a letter. Is he coming, mother?" and with eager eyes and open lips, she sat up, holding tight to her mother's arm.

"Yes, love. I have got a letter."

"Is he—is he coming?"

How the mother answered, I can hardly tell; but she did answer, and they were soon lying in each other's arms, warm with each other's tears. It was almost hard to say which was the happier.

Aaron was to be there that evening—that very evening. "Oh, mother, let me get up," said Susan.

But Mrs. Bell said no, not yet; her darling was pale and thin, and she almost wished that Aaron was not coming for another week. What if he should come and look at her, and finding her beauty gone, vanish again and seek a wife elsewhere!

So Susan lay in bed, thinking of her happiness, dozing now and again, and fearing as she waked that it was a dream, looking constantly at that drawing of his, which she kept outside upon the bed, nursing her love and thinking of it, and endeavouring, vainly endeavouring, to arrange what she would say to him.

"Mother," she said, when Mrs. Bell once went up to her, "you won't tell Hetta and Phineas, will you? Not to-day, I mean?" Mrs. Bell agreed that it would be better not to tell them. Perhaps she thought that she had already depended too much on Hetta and Phineas in the matter.

Susan's finery in the way of dress had never been extensive, and now lately, in these last sad winter days, she had thought but little of the fashion of her clothes. But when she began to dress herself for the evening, she did ask her mother with some anxiety what she had better wear. "If he loves you he will hardly see what you have on," said the mother. But not the less was she careful to smooth her daughter's hair, and make the most that might be made of those faded roses.

How Susan's heart beat,—how both their hearts beat as the hands of the clock came round to seven! And then, sharp at seven, came the knock; that same short bold ringing knock which Susan had so soon learned to know as belonging to Aaron Dunn. "Oh mother, I had better go up stairs," she cried, starting from her chair.

"No dear; you would only be more nervous."

"I will, mother."

"No, no, dear; you have not time;" and then Aaron Dunn was in the room.

She had thought much what she would say to him, but had not yet quite made up her mind. It mattered however but very little. On whatever she might have resolved, her resolution would have vanished to the wind. Aaron Dunn came into the room, and in one second she found herself in the centre of a whirlwind, and his arms were the storms that enveloped her on every side.

"My own, own darling girl," he said over and over again, as he pressed her to his heart, quite regardless of Mrs. Bell, who stood by, sobbing with joy. "My own Susan."

"Aaron, dear Aaron," she whispered. But she had already recognised the fact that for the present meeting a passive part would become her well, and save her a deal of trouble. She had her lover there quite safe, safe beyond anything that Mr. or Mrs. Beckard might have to say to the contrary. She was quite happy; only that there were symptoms now and again that the whirlwind was about to engulf her yet once more.

"Dear Aaron, I am so glad you are come," said the innocent-minded widow, as she went up stairs with him, to show him his room; and then he embraced her also. "Dear, dear mother," he said.

On the next day there was, as a matter of course, a family conclave. Hetta and Phineas came down, and discussed the whole subject of the coming marriage with Mrs. Bell. Hetta at first was not quite certain;—ought they not to inquire whether the situation was permanent?

"I won't inquire at all," said Mrs. Bell, with an energy that startled both the daughter and son-in-law. "I would not part them now; no, not if—" and the widow shuddered as she thought of her daughter's sunken eyes, and pale cheeks.

"He is a good lad," said Phineas, "and I trust she will make him a sober steady wife;" and so the matter was settled.

During this time, Susan and Aaron were walking along the Balston road; and they also had settled the matter—quite as satisfactorily.

Such was the courtship of Susan Dunn.